A Tangle of Hearts

A Shade of Vampire, Book 44

Bella Forrest

ALSO BY BELLA FORREST:

THE GENDER GAME

The Gender Game (Book 1)
The Gender Secret (Book 2)
The Gender Lie (Book 3)
The Gender War (Book 4)
The Gender Fall (Book 5)
The Gender Plan (Book 6)
The Gender End (Book 7)

THE SECRET OF SPELLSHADOW MANOR

The Secret of Spellshadow
Manor (Book 1)
The Breaker (Book 2)
The Chain (Book 3)

A SHADE OF VAMPIRE SERIES:

Series 1:
Derek & Sofia's story:

A Shade of Vampire (Book 1)
A Shade of Blood (Book 2)
A Castle of Sand (Book 3)
A Shadow of Light (Book 4)
A Blaze of Sun (Book 5)
A Gate of Night (Book 6)
A Break of Day (Book 7)

Series 2:
Rose & Caleb's story:

A Shade of Novak (Book 8)
A Bond of Blood (Book 9)
A Spell of Time (Book 10)
A Chase of Prey (Book 11)
A Shade of Doubt (Book 12)
A Turn of Tides (Book 13)
A Dawn of Strength (Book 14)
A Fall of Secrets (Book 15)
An End of Night (Book 16)

Series 3: The Shade continues with a new hero...

A Wind of Change (Book 17)
A Trail of Echoes (Book 18)
A Soldier of Shadows (Book 19)
A Hero of Realms (Book 20)
A Vial of Life (Book 21)
A Fork Of Paths (Book 22)
A Flight of Souls (Book 23)
A Bridge of Stars (Book 24)

Series 4:
A Clan of Novaks

A Clan of Novaks (Book 25)
A World of New (Book 26)
A Web of Lies (Book 27)
A Touch of Truth (Book 28)

An Hour of Need (Book 29)
A Game of Risk (Book 30)
A Twist of Fates (Book 31)
A Day of Glory (Book 32)

Series 5:
A Dawn of Guardians

A Dawn of Guardians (Book 33)
A Sword of Chance (Book 34)
A Race of Trials (Book 35)
A King of Shadow (Book 36)
An Empire of Stones (Book 37)
A Power of Old (Book 38)
A Rip of Realms (Book 39)
A Throne of Fire (Book 40)
A Tide of War (Book 41)

Series 6: A Gift of Three
A Gift of Three (Book 42)
A House of Mysteries (Book 43)
A Tangle of Hearts (Book 44)

A SHADE OF DRAGON TRILOGY :

A Shade of Dragon 1
A Shade of Dragon 2
A Shade of Dragon 3

A SHADE OF KIEV TRILOGY:

A Shade of Kiev 1
A Shade of Kiev 2
A Shade of Kiev 3

BEAUTIFUL MONSTER DUOLOGY:

Beautiful Monster 1
Beautiful Monster 2

DETECTIVE ERIN BOND
(Adult mystery/thriller)

Lights, Camera, Gone
Write, Edit, Kill

For an updated list of Bella's books, please visit her website:
www.bellaforrest.net

Join Bella's VIP email list and she'll personally send you an email
reminder as soon as her next book is out! Visit here to sign up:
www.forrestbooks.com

Contents

New Generation List

- **Aida:** daughter of Bastien and Victoria (half werewolf/half human)
- **Field:** biological son of River, adopted son of Benjamin (mix of Hawk and vampire-half-blood)
- **Jovi:** son of Bastien and Victoria (half werewolf/half human)
- **Phoenix:** son of Hazel and Tejus (sentry)
- **Serena:** daughter of Hazel and Tejus (sentry)
- **Vita:** daughter of Grace and Lawrence (part-fae/human)

Aida
[Victoria & Bastien's daughter]

The morning sun invaded our room through faded drapes and stained windows, warming the side of my face. I opened and closed my eyes a couple of times to help them adjust to the light. The damp smell was still there, and my nose crinkled. I hated this place.

I lay on the bed with my arm over my face, willing myself to sit up. In the silence, images of runes flickered before my eyes, and the previous night's chilling images of myself in the mirror crashed into me—the symbols and icons moving across my limbs like spiders. My skin crawled. I sat up and checked myself again.

My skin is clear. Not a single marking. All me, all there.

I took a deep breath and tried to shake the images from my mind. Maybe I had imagined it. Maybe the heat and exhaustion of yesterday had finally gotten to me. But, then again, maybe my reflection had been trying to tell me something, to give me a preview of what was going to happen to my body as an Oracle.

I gave myself another once-over. Still nothing. No weird black liquid on my skin. Not a single rune.

Vita shifted next to me on top of the damp sheets. She looked uncomfortable as she, too, pulled herself from a heavy sleep.

I'd probably managed a couple of hours of downtime after I'd seen myself doodled in runes in that glass cabinet. It had taken a while for me to will myself away from my own reflection and back to our room. Vita had still been asleep when my head touched the pillow, and for a brief moment, I'd envied her. She was just as screwed up as I was with this Oracle madness, but she had been able to at least sleep some of it off. I, on the other hand, had started to hallucinate.

But what if it was all real?

I looked over at her again and found her looking at me. Compassion and concern shone in her turquoise eyes. She pressed her lips together tightly, as if she wanted to say something but wasn't sure whether she should.

"In other circumstances, I'd say *Good Morning, Sunshine*," I said. I cocked my head, trying not to sound like the bundle of gloom I was inside.

Vita smiled gently, rubbed her eyes with the backs of her hands, and sat up.

"You got back late," she said.

Her words caught me by surprise. I could've sworn she'd been asleep both when I'd left and when I'd returned from my short-lived expedition through the mansion. I looked away, trying to focus my attention on the patches of blue skies and wisps of white cotton clouds outside.

"I had a hard time falling asleep," I said.

"I don't blame you." Vita sighed and fumbled with strands of her hair. It was the color of sun-kissed summer wheat fields and slightly curled from all the humidity. As quiet and reclusive as she usually was, she was always able to comfort me without words.

She'd come a long way over the past few days. We all had. From our soirée with the fae, to this life-changing insanity of Oracles, Druids, incubi, and shape-shifters—and whatever else lurked in the jungles around us—in a world where we didn't belong... and with our families stripped of the very memory of us.

Vita got out of bed and started picking out some clothes for the day.

Memories of my runes flickered through my mind, as I willed myself to tell her about what I had seen in the mirror. I just didn't want to risk worrying her unnecessarily.

She pulled out a pair of undergarments that would serve as pants, a yellowish shade of white, yet another victim of centuries past. She wrinkled her nose, apparently unhappy with her selection, but it wasn't like she had a better choice. Our sartorial whims were the least of our concerns this morning.

"Vita…"

"Hm?" She looked up at me. This was harder than I'd originally thought.

"How are you feeling?"

Her blank stare made me realize I hadn't asked the brightest question.

"I mean, with these Oracle abilities, how are you feeling? Other than visions, have you been experiencing anything else?"

Vita pulled a pale pink linen camisole from the same pile of clothes we'd recovered from the attic and examined it while she mulled over my question.

"Honestly, Aida, I'm having enough trouble with what I see," she finally said. "I'm in no rush to turn into a blind, barren, tattooed Oracle and end up in an evil overlord's fishbowl."

Fair enough.

But last night's memories nagged me like a twig poking at the back of my head.

"Yeah, I get that. I'm not eager to see where this takes us either," I said cautiously, "but I think something's happening to me, and I don't know who else to talk to about it."

My voice sounded raw in my own ears.

Vita's big bluish eyes doubled in size. She set the clothes aside on the bed and came closer to me. Concern drew a small crease between her slim eyebrows.

"What do you mean?"

I took another deep breath, one that made me feel like my lungs were about to burst and let it all out in one long sigh. I described the runes I could remember and the way they had appeared and vanished.

Sweet Vita listened quietly.

"At first I thought I imagined it," I said. "But then I saw myself in another reflective surface, and the runes were all there, and something dark was trickling out of them through my skin."

"But when you'd look down, there was nothing?" Vita asked.

I nodded and waited for her reaction.

She bent down and looked at my shoulder where it wasn't covered by my camisole. She studied my back and pulled my arms out to check them as well. She didn't speak for a full minute. In these circumstances, maybe silence was a good answer.

"It's weird," Vita murmured eventually. She passed a hand through her hair. "There definitely aren't any runes on your skin now."

"But when I looked in the mirror—"

"Wait." Vita grabbed a hand mirror from the old vanity in the corner and held it to my skin to check my reflection. I tilted my head in order to see in the mirror as well.

Nothing. Even in the mirror, my skin was clear. Relief coursed through me in hot and cold waves. I let out a tortured sigh.

Vita watched me intently. Her face said more than her words ever could; she understood.

Before I could say anything else, she hugged me tight. I hugged back. I would do anything for this girl.

"Right, so for now, let's just keep this to ourselves," Vita said. She grabbed her clothes and headed for the shower. "No need to worry the others yet. And let's be vigilant and keep an eye on each other from now on, okay?"

Her question hung in the air. She disappeared into the bathroom without waiting for my response.

I straightened my back and got out of bed. Whatever last night had been, I pushed it to the back of my head.

If any of us wanted to get out of here alive, we had our work cut out for us. There was so much still to be done.

PHOENIX
[HAZEL & TEJUS'S SON]

I tried to wash off the previous night's event with a cold shower, but it didn't do much good. Giving up, I went down to breakfast. The warm morning was hard on all of us judging by how late everyone else was.

Seeing the Daughters of Eritopia in my sleep was one of the strangest experiences of my life. And their gift to me, asking me to sacrifice myself so that the last Daughter could wake up and save us all… I'd brushed it off as just a dream, until I'd found their stone knife next to me in bed.

I sat at the breakfast table, staring at the food with unfocused eyes. My hand touched the right pocket of my pants, where the stone blade rested coldly.

I glanced up when Jovi entered the room. He didn't look great either. His fun-loving side was buried beneath a layer of grumpiness, as he grunted his way to the coffee pot. A few gulps later, he seemed to look at me with newfound interest, the color back in his cheeks.

"We need to move," he said matter-of-factly, looking at me.

"By move you mean take a peaceful stroll in the garden, or beat each other up until we feel strong again?"

I knew where he was going with this, and I needed it as much as he did. The Daughters' violet eyes, golden masks, and shivering touch couldn't be washed down with a cold shower and coffee. I needed some action. I needed to move, like Jovi said.

"I mean me beating you up." Jovi smirked and sipped loudly from his frilly porcelain cup, like a true alpha male. We didn't have much to work with in terms of dinnerware in this place, but for once it made me smile.

I stood. "Bring it on, sassy-mouth. I can't wait to watch you fall flat on your ass again."

We clinked our coffee cups as if toasting a good game and headed outside.

* * *

We chose a strip of bare garden farther away from the plantation house. The house quietly watched over us with its French windows, aged columns, and pink magnolia trees surrounding it. Even the crows watched from branches high above as we took our positions.

Jovi and I tumbled around for a while. He kicked; I blocked. He swept my legs; I swiftly rebounded and came at him with extra fire in my heels. He seemed surprisingly rested and calm in his defense, his every move almost effortlessly blocking my hits.

I, on the other hand, felt heavy and irritated. I usually had the upper hand on the guy, and now I looked like I was trying too hard, like every move I made came back to bite me.

An hour into our training, I had yet to knock him out. I threw him down a couple of times, but Jovi got up and retaliated in kind. Then again, his mind wasn't wandering off to a perfect woman, with iridescent skin and hair that seemed to be made of fire, hidden in a shell beneath a magnolia tree. He didn't have to spill his own blood in order to bring her to consciousness.

His leg caught me in the solar plexus, pushing the air from my lungs and knocking me back. At least the grass was soft and still sprinkled with cool morning dew. It felt so nice that I didn't feel like getting back up.

"What's wrong with you?"

Sighing at Jovi's question, I rose to my feet. I brushed some of the dirt and grass off and straightened my back. My muscles were getting tired, and my joints had begun their muffled protests. I resumed my fighting stance, my right foot behind me ready to act as a spring board.

"Nothing's wrong with me," I replied. I lifted my arms slowly, preparing for another attack. My breathing was a little heavy and irregular, and beads of sweat trickled down my temples.

Jovi gave me his *don't-give-me-crap* look and raised his hands in a peaceful gesture to pause our training.

"Seriously, what's up? You're way off your game," he said.

The knife in my pocket weighed too much—on my mind and body.

"I'm fine," I said, barely convincing myself.

Jovi cocked his head and lifted an eyebrow.

"I'm beating you six ways through Sunday and you never, NEVER go down this easy," he replied and crossed his arms over his chest, not ready to let it go.

I couldn't really blame him. We'd been training together for years, and he knew me better than most. I really was off my game.

I took a deep breath and looked in the distance, beyond the protective shield of the mansion, which shimmered like a nearly invisible membrane. Trees and shrubs prodded it from the swamp side, unable to penetrate. I wasn't sure whether I should tell him about my dream, about the knife. The mission was clear; it was only a question of me deciding to do it. And the sight of her, curled up in her shell, sleeping for what seemed like an eternity, tore my heart to shreds.

My hand reached into my pocket instinctively. I decided to keep the dream a secret for a little while longer. Just until I figured it out myself. I would go see her again later and then decide what the best course of action was.

"I didn't get much sleep," I muttered, brushing the thoughts off and moving my head around enough to relax my trapezius muscles and get back to knocking the smirk off Jovi's face.

"Boy, that is the lamest excuse I've ever heard you pull." He chuckled, but his smile dropped quickly as I darted at him.

I bent down in my run and slammed into his torso.

He fell backward and hit the ground, and I followed with all my weight. It was his turn to get the air knocked out of his lungs. *Quid pro quo.*

"And this is the fastest I've seen you fall so far," I grunted as we wrestled on the soft grass. Our feet pushed against the cool ground as we tried to prove that we were both perfectly okay, that this world wasn't wrong, and that we could simply play-fight our way out of anything too dark, or too sad or too serious.

Pinned beneath me, Jovi shifted his arms between mine in an attempt to gain momentum and shove me away.

A scream rang out.

We both froze and looked toward where it had come from— beyond the shield, farther to the north.

Then a different kind of scream—more like a shrill—pierced through the rustle of swamp weeds and tall grass. It came from beyond the gnarly trees that framed the muddy waters around the plantation.

A chill rushed through me.

It sounded like death.

Jovi
[Victoria & Bastien's son]

Up until that moment, my only concern had been getting Phoenix to concentrate on combat. He'd been zoned out, evasive, and dodging my questions all morning. He'd taken me by surprise during the last tackle, just enough to get me to stop worrying about him and turn my focus back to my pride, which had tumbled to the ground with me.

But the sounds of screaming brought everything to a screeching halt. Pinned beneath Phoenix in a not-so-flattering position, I swung my arms around until I knocked him off balance and broke free.

We looked at each other for a brief moment, then stretched

our necks to locate the source of the sheer agony. All we saw were old trees curling outward from the depths of the jungle bordered by dark waters, sprawling weeds, and flocks of tall grass.

"What was that?" I asked, almost out of breath.

"I don't know, but it's not good," Phoenix replied, his eyes on the jungle beyond the protective shield.

I rolled over and tuned my senses, hoping to catch the scent of whatever had screamed so horribly, but I only got a faint whiff of iron. Blood.

"Come on, Phoenix, you're the one with the better sight here!" I said.

His eyes glistened in the sunlight, a familiar expression. His True Sight must have broken through the layers of damp wood and dark green foliage, when another shrill came from between the trees. It sounded much closer than before.

"Three... There's three of them," Phoenix said, his breath cut short, as if watching a suspenseful movie unraveling in real time.

"Three of what?"

"I... I'm trying to make them out."

I rose to my knees and concentrated my gaze in the same direction, hoping to see something as well. A third scream carried echoes of unimaginable pain. It washed over us and sent tremors down my spine. My instincts were dangerously close to kicking in; I felt restless and ready to jump in and fight.

"They're being hunted," Phoenix continued, his fists clenched at his sides. "Two of them are down. They're surrounded by some really nasty creatures... Shape-shifters..."

"What do we do?" I burst to my feet. My blood boiled. Nobody deserved to get torn to shreds by mindless creatures, to get hunted down like mere animals.

"We can't go in by ourselves, Jovi," Phoenix replied, his True Sight still watching the scene. His eyes grew wide, and he took a step back.

I heard branches breaking, footsteps on the grass, and the gasping breath of someone running out of the woods.

A woman staggered out from between the gnarly old trees and made her way toward the waters. She looked young, her body covered in tight animal skins and what looked like red and silver paint. Her hair was long, ink black, and tangled with twigs and leaves.

She held her shoulder as if in pain and jumped over a thick, empty tree trunk.

A grotesque creature reached out from behind her and clawed at her leg mid-jump.

She screamed and fell forward, rolling into the water.

Shadows moved quickly between the trees. Wails erupted from the darkness of the jungle, the sadistic squeals of animals enjoying the hunt. The woman was the prey.

"We have to do something," I said, my chest heaving.

She struggled to get out of the swamp, seemingly stuck. Her frustrated grunts fused with pain as she desperately fought to free herself from whatever had her trapped.

"Once we're past the shield, we're vulnerable to whatever's coming after her." Phoenix said.

My lid blew off instantly. "So what do we do? Let her die?"

The creature emerged from behind the trunk, hairless and hideous.

We both froze.

It moved swiftly along the patches of dirt in the brown waters on its knuckles and feet. Its fangs were sharp and white, and strips of muscle held the jaw in place.

More screams shot from the woods, adding layer upon layer of raw pain and horror. The other two women were being torn to shreds, and I couldn't let that happen to the one left standing. I just couldn't.

I looked at Phoenix. "Sorry," I mumbled and ran straight for the woman stuck in the swamp.

"Don't! Jovi!" he shouted.

I couldn't watch her get ripped apart by shape-shifters. Eritopia wasn't my favorite place, and I had no intention of standing back and letting its psychotic nature ruin another life. I sprinted, jumping over the mounds and boulders scattered across the patch of land beyond the shield.

"Hey!" I shouted, hoping to distract the beast. It was closer to the wounded woman now. She turned her head and saw me. Her eyes widened and I was struck by their peculiar shades of green and gold.

The creature saw me and rose to its feet. The closer I got, the uglier it looked with bones poking out in all the wrong places and translucent skin stretching and then rippling over raw muscle. The beast suddenly morphed into me.

The realization of what I was facing stopped me in my tracks. I was looking at a very disturbing version of myself.

"That's just…sick," I said.

I shook the thought off. I had to save the woman. I wasn't ready to hear her screams as shape-shifters ripped her apart.

I darted toward her and leaped into the murky waters.

PHOENIX
[HAZEL & TEJUS'S SON]

My heart jumped into my throat as Jovi plunged into the swamp. I cursed under my breath and ran after him. His chivalry was about to get him killed, and I couldn't stand back and watch that happen. The safety of the protective shield be damned!

I reached them just as the shape-shifter was about to jump in after Jovi and the woman. I shouted at it, hoping to distract the creature long enough for Jovi to get the woman out of there. Diversion was our only hope.

The beast looked at me, and I was genuinely creeped out by its resemblance to Jovi. Its skin rippled once more, and before I could blink I was looking at myself—the same black hair, dark eyes, and athletic build, but there was something feral, something inherently evil, about my lookalike. It hissed and bared its fangs at me, ready for a fight.

"Get her out of there, Jovi!" I shouted at my reckless, knight-in-shining-armor friend. Jovi jerked at the underwater vine the woman had gotten tangled in.

"Believe it or not, I'm trying!" he yelled back. He drew a lungful of air and dove to the bottom, leaving me to face off with the monstrous copy of myself.

I resumed my focus on the shape-shifter. *Diversion. Right.*

I trained my energy on the shape-shifter and reached out to its mind. My eyes burned as I tried to capture its will and force it into submission, but I hit a black wall. The creature's mind was either blank or impossible to infiltrate.

Damn. Mind control won't work.

It hissed at me and took a few steps forward. Its stride was arrogant, and it sneered at my inability to subdue it, like it expected me to crumble after one failed attempt.

I stood my ground, ready to syphon it to its knees. I wasn't in top shape after the previous day and night, and I had to work harder to aim and capture the shape-shifter's energy, but I opened myself up and focused with all that I had.

The creature faltered.

It's working.

A rancid heat slipped into my temples, and bile burned the

back of my throat. Whatever I was syphoning out of the creature was incredibly toxic. I had to stop. The shape-shifter cackled, as if aware of what it was doing to me.

I looked over at Jovi, who still struggled to get the woman out.

I spotted a dozen more shape-shifters coming out of the jungle, leaning on their knuckles, their disgusting faces smeared with what looked like silver paint.

"Damn."

They crept closer, unfurling their bodies at their waists and transforming into a dozen creepy versions of myself. It seemed to be their favorite game, using their ability to draw out unsuspecting prey and confuse their opponent.

My chest burned with fear. What were my choices?

The creatures swiftly formed an arch before me. Their hissing clouded my ears, and their eyes glinted. They could tear me apart in seconds.

I pushed a barrier of energy out, but the toxic syphoning had taken its toll. My sentry game was weak. I drew a deep breath and pushed again, sourcing every ounce of energy I had left. But the pulse barely nudged them. My barrier building wasn't going to get us out of this.

No other choice.

My breath grew short. The shape-shifters closed in on me. My hand went for my pocket, fingers clutching the final solution—the knife. The twine wrapped around the handle added friction to my tight grip as I drew the blade from my pocket.

The beasts hissed in my ears. I felt their hot breath mere yards from me. It was now or never. I dodged their clawed hands and wove frantically between them.

I couldn't be still for even a split second. I ducked from side to side, blocking their hits and slashing at them with the knife. Dark brown blood seeped from their arms and chests.

The knife felt light in my hand, and my arm drew short arches around me. Down left, up right. Down right, up left. Repeated at different angles. Ducking faster and faster to keep myself out of the shape-shifters' reach. I slit a neck and the creature fell back, clutching its throat.

I could do this. I could. But then my feet were swept from underneath me, and everything flickered into darkness.

JOVI
[Victoria & Bastien's son]

Her left ankle was tangled with thick black vines beneath the water, while her other leg had been slashed at by the shape-shifter during her jump. She was in terrible pain, and I couldn't leave her. Her right shoulder slumped, and she couldn't move her right arm at all. She clung to me with the other. I dove, accidentally gulping mouthfuls of muddy water in my effort to set her free.

I pulled at the vine's knots. One strand came loose from the tangle. I jerked at the rest of it, unraveling enough to free her.

When I looked up, I prayed to see Phoenix still standing. My chest constricted as I watched him fall.

"PHOENIX!" I yelled.

I shouted at the creatures, and so did the woman in my arms. We both seemed to know what we had to do to get Phoenix out of there—provided we survived.

The monsters fell back on their knees and knuckles, morphing down to their original figures of nearly-transparent skin and bony limbs. They poised to dive right into Phoenix's chest, their claws and fangs ready to gore him to death.

I bellowed again and rushed through the water. My heart throbbed against my ribs, but adrenaline fueled my desperate attempt to reach them before they could kill Phoenix.

Water splashed behind me as the woman followed. It occurred to me to be impressed by her resilience and determination, but the thought passed. My friend was about to die.

The shape-shifters nudged each other furiously, as if arguing over who got to make the killing. Phoenix lay unconscious on the hard mound rising through the middle of the swamp.

I shouted again and again, trying to draw their attention away from him. "HEY! Fresh meat! Right here!"

"Hey! Hey! Yah!" the woman shouted behind me.

One of the creatures looked over its shoulder at us. The others continued to hiss and push at each other. I would have given anything to go wolf and rip them apart, one by one.

A dark shadow descended on the group. A mass of muscle

and black wings rammed into the shape-shifters, throwing them out like pins in a bowling game. Field was a gift from the sky in that moment.

He punched left and right and kicked his way through the jumble of hairless beasts. They scratched and wailed as they were separated from their prey.

I froze in the water with the woman behind me and watched as Field tore through the shape-shifters. They were relentless in their attacks. Nevertheless, his wings and speed gave him the advantage.

I tugged at the woman, and we rushed back to the other edge of the water. I pulled myself up and dragged her with me.

I paused and saw Field take a few hits before he landed on top of Phoenix, grabbed him, and spread his wings out so violently that he knocked the shape-shifters backward. It gave him the short opening he needed to pull Phoenix out and fly back toward the mansion.

The woman crawled out of the swamp and tried to stand and run, but her leg gave out, and she collapsed. Blood pounded through my veins like rivers of fire, and I felt my pulse throbbing in my fingertips.

This was our chance.

I swept her up in my arms and ran as fast as I could. She struggled, but I held her tightly and kept sprinting toward the shimmer of the protective shield.

Behind us, the shape-shifters screamed and tumbled through the undergrowth, rushing after us. I heard their feet rustle over the grass and their howls of hunger and frustration.

Breath brushed over my calf as I ran, as one of them tried to take a bite out of me.

I sped up and passed through the shield.

Field glided a few yards from the ground and slammed into the mansion's front door. It splintered on impact.

Leave it to Field to make a theatrical entrance.

I looked over my shoulder and saw the shape-shifters crashing against the protective shield, and I couldn't help quietly sending out my gratitude to the Daughters of Eritopia for the shield. The creatures howled and kept trying to advance, but the Daughters' magic zapped them backward.

My feet didn't stop, but the adrenaline vanished. My knees gave out mid-run and I tripped. I saw the ground approach me with dangerous speed and spun a one-eighty to protect the woman from the fall.

I landed hard on my back and slid through the grass, not letting her go.

She whimpered in my arms, but I held on tightly.

My shoulder blades burned from the friction, and her weight pressed against my chest. My lungs felt empty, stuck to my ribs.

And yet I looked up, pleased to still see the blue sky with wisps of white clouds above.

VitA
[Grace and Lawrence's daughter]

I had a lot on my mind as I left our room and made my way downstairs for breakfast. The shower had cooled me off a little, but I still couldn't stop myself from revisiting previous visions of the Nevertide Oracle.

Why had she sent us to the Daughters? Had her intentions been skewed? Had Azazel manipulated us through her? It didn't make much sense, since the Daughters of Eritopia had no interest in playing his sick games, but Draven still lost his eyes in the process. I couldn't wrap my head around this systematic cruelty.

What was the purpose of all of this?

We didn't get anything out of the visit except for some vague notion of the last Daughter's awakening. How were we supposed to wake her? We only got more questions.

My feet brushed over the last few steps. I shook my head.

What does the Oracle want from us?

Jovi's imminent death squeezed my heart and tied knots in my stomach. What steps were we taking that would lead us to that specific outcome? What could we do differently?

I reached the ground floor, the old planks creaking beneath me, and once again envisioned the Nevertide Oracle floating quietly in her sphere. I remembered her face, pale in the water.

Heat rose to my temples, and everything went white. My body felt weightless, like a stream pouring through the abyss. Darkness closed in from all sides, and the white light concentrated into a tunnel that stretched ahead of me.

I lost myself to the vision.

* * *

At the end of the tunnel was one of the rooms of the plantation house. The heavy cream curtains were drawn, and I could see the fine centuries-old embroidery highlighted where the pearly moon cast its milky light. The tourmaline sky was clear and riddled with stars.

The walls were covered in the same faded pink wallpaper, torn and peeled off here and there. There was plenty of furniture around—a couple of mahogany dressers, a heavy chest of drawers, and a small vanity table tucked away in a corner. Clothes were strewn all over the floor. The bed I lay on felt surprisingly comfortable.

I was enveloped in a pleasant and comforting warmth, molded to another body. I looked to my right and saw Bijarki. His arms were wrapped around me, his face nuzzling the hollow space between my neck and shoulder. His fingers drew circles on my bare skin beneath the linen sheets.

The clothes on the floor were ours.

It felt natural to be there. He moaned in his sleep, his lips moving and kissing my collarbone, sending waves of soft heat into my stomach. His silvery skin glistened under the moonlight pouring through the window, and I relished the sensations he offered me, even while he slept.

Our bodies fit perfectly together. Our hearts beat next to each other in a peculiar unison. And I didn't want the moment to end. I could've stayed there forever.

Then, the wall exploded inward, shooting splinters and glass shards all over the room. They scratched my skin and tore my lover from his sleep.

The cool night wind blew inside and brought with it Destroyers atop their winged black horses. They rumbled into the room, their ghostly wails sending chills down my spine. I froze in my little spot in the bed, and Bijarki tried to shield my body with his.

They pulled us apart. I watched, helplessly, as they dragged him away, leather whips coiled around his throat and arms. He shouted my name over and over, his eyes wide and filled with dread.

One of the Destroyers slithered off its horse and rushed toward me, its crooked fingers curled around a burlap sack. I screamed as loudly as I could. How had they been able to breach the protective shield?

I screamed for Bijarki, for myself, for my friends who slept under the false assumption that we were safe in the mansion.

A snake tail wrapped itself around my throat, slick and cold and heavy. The burlap sack covered my head, and everything went black.

* * *

I came to, gasping for air. My fingers desperately tried to pull the snake tail away from my throat. My body contorted with panic.

A pair of arms held me down. A gentle voice told me that everything was okay.

My eyes came back into focus. I was at the bottom of the stairs, and I could see the plastered ceiling, the stuffed animals with beady eyes, the dusty curtains on tall east windows.

Bijarki looked down at me, his hands pressing my shoulders

into the floor.

My lungs struggled to catch up. Sweat glued my hair to my forehead. I felt sticky and hot and cold at the same time. I tried to take deep breaths to return to some semblance of calm.

Bijarki's voice was smooth, his eyebrows scrunched into a concerned frown. The corners of his mouth turned down, his firm lips tight.

"It was just a vision, Vita," he said, his voice soothing. "Take it easy."

"What… What are you doing here?" I asked, instantly remembering that I had been specific in my request the other day. "I told you to stay away!"

I sat up and shuffled backward on my heels and palms until my back hit a wall. Unless I could sink into it, that was as far as I could get from Bijarki.

What the hell were you doing in my bed?

He watched me with a mixture of befuddlement and humor, irritating me even more. What could be so funny when I'd just had visions of myself naked next to him like it was the most natural thing in the world?

"I heard a thump from upstairs, and when I came out, you were on the floor here, mid-seizure," he replied.

A few moments passed while I analyzed everything. I'd been thinking about the Nevertide Oracle and, the next thing I knew, I saw myself with Bijarki while Destroyers broke into the mansion.

Destroyers invaded the mansion.

"Just keep your distance, please." I felt the need to reiterate, maybe more for myself than for him.

"As you can see, I'm staying away, but don't expect me to ignore you if you fall flat on your face with another vision," Bijarki replied, his voice low and his jaw visibly tense. "Are you all right now?"

I stood. My cheeks flamed. Heat clogged my throat. My body longed for his embrace, and I crossed my arms as though a shield would help. I was still too close to him. I'd just felt his skin on mine; a million miles didn't seem far enough away.

"I'm fine," I muttered. I walked past him and dashed into the breakfast room. Maybe a few gallons of water and the presence of my friends would cool everything down.

The door closed behind me with a resounding thud. No one was there. *Ugh.* I went straight for the water jug and gulped down a full glass, expecting Bijarki to come in and turn the heat up again.

Three glasses later, he had yet to emerge.

I took a deep breath and looked over to the door. Maybe he'd already come in and was standing there like the incubus stalker that he was. *What the hell was I doing in bed with him?*

He never came.

And why don't I like the fact that he isn't here now?

I could punch myself. I'd been so closed off in the past, so afraid to show my true self to anyone, that I'd gotten too comfortable in my little shell. Then came Eritopia and this Oracle business, flooding my mind with the wildest visions of myself. The future basically smacked me in the face, telling me that my introvert nature was about to get the jaws-of-life treatment.

I'd told the incubus to stay away from me. I'd left his side, even when all he'd done was show genuine concern. And when he didn't come after me, I sulked like a little girl.

Ugh, Vita.

SERENA
[HAZEL AND TEJUS'S DAUGHTER]

I woke up to pain shooting through my back. I sat up. Sunlight hit my face. My spine crackled like an old twig, sending tiny spasms through the muscles attached to it. I rubbed my eyes and allowed myself the loudest yawn I could summon from the bottom of my compressed lungs. As cramped as it was, I missed the bed I normally shared with the girls. The armchair in Draven's room was far worse.

I'm in Draven's room.

The realization hit me hard. I looked at the bed and found the Druid sitting up, quiet and motionless. His sand-colored hair was ruffled in various directions. The bandage around his eyes was a grim reminder of what had happened the day before. The runes on his chest were dark brown crusts on otherwise perfectly smooth, tanned skin.

Judging by the smirk on his face, I figured he'd heard my booming yawn. My cheeks simmered, and I waited for him to say something. A few moments passed. I stared at him, taking in the heavy lines of his torso and strong arms, the sculptural blade of his nose, and his lips, arched in a half-smile. I opened my mouth but couldn't think of anything to say.

"Thank you for staying overnight." Draven's voice was husky but gentle.

That was unexpected. I cleared my throat and nodded, then remembered that he couldn't see.

"It was the least I could do," I replied.

Another awkwardly long moment passed. Birds chirped outside in the garden. His smirk persisted.

"It's ironic how quiet you are right now," he said.

"What do you mean?"

"Usually you're a bundle of questions before the sun even comes up, making my existence ten times more difficult, yet now you're silent. If it weren't so relaxing, I'd say it's odd. Downright uncharacteristic. Even cause for concern. Are you sick, maybe?" Draven went on, still smiling.

In my still-bleary state, his words were a sharp reminder of what I had to do for my own, my brother's, and my friends' sakes. Drill the Druid for information. Get closer to him, find out more about him, about his kind, about the Oracles, the Destroyers, Azazel, and everything else that was so fundamentally characteristic yet so wrong about Eritopia. Learn how it had gotten to this point, who or what he really was, and what we could do to stop all the carnage and destruction and rescue ourselves.

I took a deep breath and reminded myself to tackle my mission systematically, one question at a time, provided he was in the mood, of course.

"Speaking of which—" I started and saw him shift immediately, "the Daughters mentioned that the last Daughter must be awoken in order to save Eritopia from Azazel. How do we do that?"

Draven let out a tortuous sigh. I watched the runes on his chest move up and then down. Even with his injuries, he was so handsome that my breath got stuck in my throat.

Focus, Serena.

"I should've kept my mouth shut and enjoyed the silence," Draven said. "Serves me right."

He scooted to the side of the bed, a grimace of pain twisting his features. He was holding his grunts in, unwilling to show weakness. His legs shifted so that his feet hung in the air as he pushed himself to the edge of the bed.

"What are you doing?" I asked, alarm flaring in my voice.

"I'm pretty sure I'm the blind one in this room, but in case you can't see what I'm doing, I'll explain. I am getting out of bed," he said.

"Draven, you've just been through a major ordeal, you're injured, and, as you so clearly put it yourself, you are blind," I interjected. "You should rest some more and let your body recover. You're of no use to anyone like this, not even yourself!"

His feet touched the floor. I shifted in the armchair, wanting to help him.

"You don't know me very well, Serena, but I'm sure you'll understand soon enough. I'm not useless, and I'm not out of the game. I need to move. I need to do whatever I can to keep everyone safe," he said, then his voice dropped. "Especially you."

I frowned. I wasn't exactly sure what to make of his last statement, so I decided not to directly address it. "Don't be stubborn," I countered. "You're still injured. Just stay in bed until the Daughters give you your eyesight back. We're safe here for now!"

"I'm not going to wait for anything. I was quite specific when I said that we're running out of time. Whether I can see or not, that isn't going to change. Time moves on." Draven stood up.

"Draven, don't!" I darted away from my chair and reached him in a split second with the intention of pushing him back on the bed and nagging him until he stayed put. I expected some kind of opposition when I pushed him, so I added some extra strength to my motion, but he didn't resist.

He fell back on the bed, and I was too late to stop myself. I landed on top of him. My palms pressed against his shoulders, and millions of little jolts charged from my fingertips to my core. The feeling of him beneath me was electric, dangerous.

We both reacted like the opposing forces we were supposed to be. We scrambled away from each other. I jumped back and tried to catch my breath. He moved his head around, as if trying to hear me, to figure out where I'd gone.

I cleared my throat again and decided to plead with him instead. Anything to get our minds off of what had just happened.

"Draven, please…take it easy."

My whole body trembled from having been so close to his. Then, it hit me.

"I'll help you. I owe you this much," I said and softened my voice. "I'll stay by your side, I'll get you whatever you need, I'll do everything I can, just…don't rush into it."

He seemed to process my request. He moved his head, as if looking to his side, enough for the morning sun to touch his face. The corner of his mouth moved upwards, while his ribcage still struggled with his ragged breath.

I couldn't have been that heavy.

"You won't leave my side?" he asked and, for a brief moment, I felt like I was talking to the little boy who had stolen Elissa's diary so she would play with him.

I couldn't help the sigh of surrender that tumbled out of me.

"Whatever I can do to help, Draven. I owe you this much," I honey glazed my voice. I had to stay close, I had to get him to open up and spill what he knew, and I had to prepare myself for the whole truth, no matter how unpleasant or downright horrifying it was.

He took his time with a resolution. I cursed him in my mind, since he wasn't making this any easier. To be fair, his entire presence wasn't making it easier for me. My gaze kept running over his features, his wounded chest, his hair, his lips.

At least he can't see me looking.

And just then, as if having read my freaking mind, he straightened his back, and moved his head to fully face me. I mirrored his movements almost out of instinct and stood straight, holding my breath.

"I can't stay in bed," he concluded, almost deflating my resolve, "but I'll accept your help."

Good. I further cemented my argument. "I'll be your eyes, until you get yours back."

"Oh, you'll be so much more than that." He almost laughed when he said that, showing me a side of him that I'd only glimpsed once. "You'll have to put up with me. I'll lean on you. I'll need to feel you near me at all times."

Where is he going with this? Annoyingly, my cheeks warmed

again.

"And, most importantly, you'll have to listen to my every word, obey my every command, and—"

"Okay, I get the picture," I cut him off, unwilling to give him any more satisfaction. "All right, I'll let you get out of bed and—"

A massive bang ripped through the house downstairs and interrupted our little back and forth.

Glass shattered. Heavy objects smashed against the wood, like someone had thrown a dresser, a piano, and a sofa down the stairs all at once.

The rumble echoed and froze my senses. Draven stilled.

Then Field's tortured voice cried out like an alarm.

SERENA
[HAZEL AND TEJUS'S DAUGHTER]

Draven instantly stood up. Without asking for permission, I grabbed his hand and placed it on my shoulder to guide him out of the bedroom. Grunts and moans coming from the foyer made me want to run. I tried hard to keep myself under control, at least until I reached the source of the ruckus.

"Who's there?" I shouted as we turned the corner toward the main entrance.

Technically speaking, there was no main entrance anymore. The double doors had been torn to shreds and splintered all over the place. Broken glass was sprinkled everywhere. On top of the entire mess, Field had collapsed over Phoenix, his wings spread out and twitching. He must have been in a considerable amount of pain, but the sight of my unconscious brother hit me with a force to rival their crash into the mansion.

I rushed toward them, leaving Draven to lean against the wall.

"Phoenix!" I shouted.

I rolled Field off of him, quickly glancing over the Hawk's body. I noticed a multitude of scratches and cuts drawing beads of blood all over his torso and arms. He'd been in a serious fight.

Phoenix, on the other hand, was still. I ran my hands over him in a panic, and stilled when I found the back of his head sticky with blood and already forming a lump.

I gasped.

"What's going on?" Draven asked behind me.

Groaning, Field raised his head and shook it. He paled at the sight of Phoenix and jumped to his knees, seemingly forgetting about his own pain. He pulled his shirt off, rolled it, and placed it under my brother's head.

"We need to put pressure there," he said.

"Phoenix, please!" I gasped, willing him to come to consciousness.

Draven had gone quiet by the wall, probably trying to listen in and understand what was happening. I could barely bring myself to respond to him with my brother limp in my arms.

Motion entered my field of vision where the door used to be. I turned my head and saw Jovi stagger in with a woman leaning against him. She looked young and wore animal skins tightly wrapped around her torso and hips. What I assumed was some kind of red and silver war paint peaked through beneath layers of dirt and shredded grass all over her body.

It was only when I saw the wounds on her leg and shoulder that I realized she wasn't just a woman but a female incubus—a succubus. The silvery war paint was, in fact, the color of her skin. Her iridescent blood seeped from her injuries, creating quite the contrast against Jovi's muscular frame. They'd clearly both taken a tumble. What had happened? The facts weren't lining up in my mind with my usual speed.

"What happened? Who's that?" I heard myself asking everyone and no one.

"What's going on—?" Bijarki rushed in from another room, soon joined by Vita. His question broke off once he took in the entire scene.

Vita gasped and fell to her knees next to me in front of Phoenix.

"We need some help here," Jovi grunted.

Bijarki clearly recognized the woman as one of his own kind, and an instinctual frown darkened his face.

She didn't look thrilled to see him either.

Still, he moved over and took on some of the succubus's weight, as she reluctantly leaned against both Jovi and him for support. A grimace shot across her face when she tried to move her arm, but Bijarki held her tight, his hand firm around her waist.

Aida's gasp caught my attention as she joined the chaos and took in the damage. I maintained pressure on my brother's head, while Aida took Field aside with trembling hands. She pushed him back to lean against a side table that hadn't been pulverized during his landing. His wings slowly retracted behind him, as Aida tried to ascertain what his injuries were. More cuts became visible on Field's body.

Vita stood frozen from the number of things going on at once.

"Phoenix, can you hear me?" I called to my unconscious brother. Tears welled up in my throat. "Phoenix, please!"

Draven's voice boomed out, piercing through our individual panic attacks.

"What is going on here?" he shouted over all of us, and we halted our pleas and gasps and mindless fumbling.

Bijarki kept his focus on the succubus woman, still eyeing her with suspicion.

Jovi was the first to speak. "Shape-shifters," he blurted, recovering his breath. "They were after a group of women... I had to... We had to do something... The shape-shifters caught two of them, but I couldn't let them kill this one too..."

Draven's head moved, as if acknowledging an unknown presence in the room. "Woman? This one?" he asked, his voice cool and even.

"A succubus," Bijarki interjected, placing an unfavorable accent on the word. She didn't seem to like his tone either, but she looked too weak to protest.

"We had to help her," Jovi insisted. "She was stuck in the swamp. One of those freaks was about to pounce on her. I jumped in to get her, and Phoenix tried to distract the beasts. He held his own for a while but then fell and hit his head."

I stared at him with a mixture of awe and horror as he finished explaining what had transpired.

There was a pause before Draven spoke again. He'd most likely calculated all possible outcomes in that silence while my mind raced with fear for my brother's life.

"You left the shield to save a succubus? You have very little regard for your own safety, obviously," he replied.

"Can you save the preaching for later?" I burst out. "My brother is hurt, and he needs help!" I could no longer hold in the tears, and they streamed down my cheeks in rivers.

On hearing me, Draven's expression softened, and he straightened his shoulders.

"Bijarki," he called out to the incubus, who—as if reading Draven's mind—left the succubus with Jovi and went to offer his shoulder as support to the Druid.

"The succubus is badly injured," Bijarki noted. "She's part of a tribe, judging by the color on her."

"What about the others?" Draven asked.

I felt my blood rising up to my temples as I stood helpless with my brother's head in my bloody hands.

"They're dead," Jovi replied, struggling to stand on his own shaky knees and support the wounded succubus.

"Guys! Phoenix!" I barked at them, stuck between fury and desperation.

"We need to get them all downstairs to the basement, where they can get the right treatment," Draven replied calmly. "Aida," he called out.

Aida looked over her shoulder. Field was hunched on the floor, lethargic and visibly weakened from his injuries.

"You deal with Field. I'll tell you what to do downstairs. Help him up." Draven started assigning roles and responsibilities with the proficiency of an army general. "Vita."

Vita sat in front of me, trembling from the shock of everything that was happening.

"I need you to help me get downstairs," Draven continued. "Bijarki will help Serena take Phoenix into the basement, and Jovi can bring the succubus down himself. He saved her, so he's responsible for her."

Vita pulled herself up and went over to Draven, placing his hand on her shoulder.

Bijarki joined me and helped pull Phoenix up from the floor.

All I could do was pray to every single entity in Eritopia

for my brother's life. I held him from one side, Bijarki held him from the other, and we carried him down to the basement.

AIDA
[Victoria & Bastien's daughter]

My mouth was dry and my heart pounded in my chest. Field didn't look as bad as Phoenix, but he didn't inspire much positivity either.

Field couldn't take his eyes off Phoenix as Bijarki and Serena carried him out of the foyer.

I, on the other hand, couldn't take my eyes off of Field. He moved to get up, and I pulled myself back, giving him space. I wasn't sure he needed my help, and I didn't want to ram myself down his throat like some kind of nagging girlfriend. He stood and seemed to handle himself pretty well.

I felt relieved. He was going to be okay.

His hair was ruffled, and his bare chest was scratched and cut all over by shape-shifters, but he still towered over me confidently.

I followed the rest of the group, expecting him to accompany me.

Something thudded.

I turned and found him fallen to his knees, trying to get back up. I cursed myself for thinking he'd be okay and hurried to him. I drew in an anchoring breath and touched his broad, firm shoulders. I had tried so hard to keep my distance from him and not come across as the little wolf-girl with a crush, but it seemed like Eritopia was bent on throwing him into my arms.

Field looked up and tried to put on a reassuring smile, but his hazy expression made it obvious that he was seeing double or triple. I figured he was more amused at seeing two or three of me at once than he was happy to see me.

I helped him stand back up, and he put an arm around my shoulders.

"I'm sorry. I'm heavy." He grunted from the pain and held his side with his other arm.

"Let's just get you downstairs," I replied and helped him toward the basement.

He hissed at every other step and struggled not to lean on me too much. I didn't mind, though. I was strong and perfectly capable of supporting him. I was also determined not to come across as a fragile little girl—not in front of Field.

It took us a few minutes to stagger down the staircase, but eventually we made it into the basement. I looked around. Vita and Serena were with Phoenix and Draven, while Jovi and Bijarki stood by the succubus. Her presence made me wary—none of us seemed to know yet if we could trust her, not even Bijarki.

I didn't want Field anywhere near her. We didn't know who she was, what she wanted, or how she'd stumbled upon the mansion, and I definitely wasn't going to allow her to look at him.

I shook that last thought out of my head. I sounded overprotective and jealous.

Snap out of it.

We reached one of the spare beds and, after a few grunts, I managed to get Field to lie down. His face was ashen from the pain and, as I looked over his magnificent torso, I could see why. A dark, reddish purple bruise bloomed on half of his ribcage. Either broken or cracked ribs, for sure. It broke my heart to see him this way.

I rushed to get some water and clean towels and began dabbing his wounds, one at a time.

He was quiet, and I was grateful for that. I bit into my lower lip and moved slowly in order to cause him as little discomfort as possible. Seeing him in pain clawed at my insides and made me angry at him for his lack of regard for his own safety and at myself for not being able to keep a clear head.

"I'll be okay," Field said, as he watched me press a wet towel on the deep cuts on his shoulder.

I shot him an irritated look, channeling all of my frustration into it.

"Yeah, but let's hope the pain will remind you to be less of an idiot next time and not fly through doors," I replied and bit my lower lip again.

"I had no other choice, Aida." My name rolled off his tongue in a way that made me stop what I was doing and take a quick, involuntary breath.

I quickly averted my attention to the scratches on his abdomen, near the horrific bruise that got worse with every minute.

"Yeah, well, maybe try a little harder next time and remember there are people who care for you and can't stand to see you hurt!" I snapped, trying to make my tone deep and unforgiving.

His frown made me regret it. He appeared to be genuinely touched by my words, and I felt bad for being so sharp.

After all, what would I have done if I'd seen Phoenix knocked out by a bunch of shape-shifters? I probably would've wound up way worse. I didn't have wings. I couldn't even turn into a wolf. I would've been useless.

He seemed to notice me soften up a little bit. I could never really hide myself from him, no matter how hard I tried. His eyes twinkled as he watched my trembling hands trying to clean a deeper cut right above his belly button. I had a hard time keeping myself focused on my task with my knuckles brushing over his abs. They were firm and tense beneath his skin.

"You seem to be taking this very hard," he quipped.

I swallowed. *Keep your cool.*

"We're in this together. What would you expect me to do? Shrug it off and let septicemia take care of it?" I replied, somewhat proud of myself for my fast comeback.

"We are in this together. I just didn't realize you felt so strongly about my wellbeing."

Field's counterattack made me freeze. My eyes fixated on a little patch of skin, just above his belt, where a shape-shifter had viciously clawed.

I looked at him, and his expression further demolished my resolve. I could feel my tough-girl talk crumbling with each passing second. His dark, serious eyes seemed to peer right into my soul.

"I'm just worried, Field, that's all," I muttered, my voice pinned in my throat. I couldn't focus on cleaning his wounds while he had that constant effect on me. And my wolf senses be damned, he smelled amazing—a mixture of musk and wilderness and mountain air that I'd learned over the years to instantly assign to Field as his natural scent.

All I had to do was finish cleaning his wounds and get as far away from him as possible. I looked away and resumed my task, dampening the towel in fresh water and dabbing at his cuts one at a time.

I tried to tune him out, but I couldn't help but register the sound of his heart beating. The rhythm echoed in the pit of my stomach, and my hands had a hard time obeying my brain. I felt him watching me.

Don't look at him.

Of course I did. And there it was, his signature smirk with that killer dimple. An unfamiliar warmth twinkled in his eyes as he watched me.

"What's so funny?" I snapped.

An excruciatingly long second passed before Field decided to share his thoughts. "I just…we never really do this, huh?" he replied, his voice low.

"Do what? You slam into doors and me nurse you while cursing my existence? Yeah, it's a first, for sure," I shot back and pressed a little too hard into one of the cuts.

He groaned from the pain, and I quickly dabbed the same spot with fresh water to soothe him. He chuckled, tempting me to press even harder, but I couldn't bring myself to be so vindictive with a man who had nearly gotten himself killed to save his friend.

"No, I mean, talk. Just be near one another and talk," he said, continuing to bombard my defenses.

My cheeks caught fire. *What is happening here?*

"There's not much talking going on right now. It's just you being delirious and me trying to make sure you don't get blood poisoning," I persisted.

"We should try this again in different circumstances." He smiled at me.

It was a soft, endearing side of him that I had never seen before. I wasn't sure whether it was just his loss of blood speaking or whether he was warming up to me, but I felt like I was melting, one inch at a time.

My skin kept touching his while I daubed his wounds, and all I could do was count my breaths silently, doing my best to keep a straight face and not give in to a dangerous instinct that pushed me to get closer.

I'd been head over heels for this man for as long as I could remember. It was innocent and adorable at first, but then I grew up and found it difficult to look him in the eyes, knowing that each night another woman held him close and whispered words of love into his ear.

Now that Maura was gone, I felt incredibly vulnerable in front of him. She'd been my reason to keep pushing him out of my mind, to tell myself that there was no way he would ever really see me.

Yet here he was, lying on that bed, his body literally in my hands, looking at me with an expression that I'd never seen from him.

Jovi
[Victoria & Bastien's son]

The reality of what had just happened started to sink in by the time I reached the basement and helped the woman onto one of the beds. Serena and Vita were trying to wake Phoenix up. Bijarki left Draven leaning against a cabinet next to Phoenix's bed and joined me.

I felt horrible. My body hurt down to my fingers and toes, but it was the sight of Phoenix, unresponsive and so badly injured, that tore me apart. I had been the crazy one. I had left the safety of the mansion to rescue a complete stranger.

He'd jumped in and faced off against a dozen shape-shifters so I could get out of that swamp alive with a creature we knew nothing about.

A succubus, as Bijarki had so quickly identified.

I watched as the incubus retrieved water, herbs, and towels to treat her wounds. She'd taken quite the beating in that jungle. Long, deep cuts ran from her shoulder down her arm and down one of her legs.

She clearly didn't like us much. She could probably feel that we didn't trust her. She tried to push Bijarki away, hissing at him like Lucifer on a bad day.

Bijarki didn't pay much attention to her. His focus was aimed at her wounds. Her skin was silvery like his, and her blood resembled liquid mercury as it seeped from the cuts. Her body was a sight to behold, even beneath the layers of red paint and swamp dirt. Her shoulders were wide, while her hourglass figure was toned with heavy training.

Her hair was long, the color of the night sky. Even tangled with twigs and leaves and mud, it preserved its specific brilliance. Her lips were full and seemed soft, and I leaned in, tempted to touch them.

"Jovi, snap out of it," Bijarki said, tearing me out of my silent analysis of the stranger I'd risked everything to save. "Be careful. You don't know what she's capable of."

Guilt washed over me anew. I'd risked my friend's life for her. If he never woke up, I wouldn't be able to forgive myself.

"Get away from me," the woman growled at us and pushed

Bijarki away. Her voice was hypnotic, a low and guttural melody that sounded alarm bells in the back of my head.

"We're trying to help you," I said. My voice sounded weak, and I mentally slapped myself for my inability to come across as firm and unyielding in front of this stranger with unknown intentions.

"Sit still, succubus," Bijarki snapped, "unless you want to crawl out of here while bleeding to death."

That worked better than my pathetic attempt at calming her down. She stilled but kept her stunning body stiff, while Bijarki cleaned the cuts and applied a mixture of nasty smelling herbs down their entire length. I could tell he had done this before, perhaps one too many times.

I looked at her and found her watching me, her eyes wide with a mixture of gold and green, shadowed by long, black eyelashes. I took one of the damp towels and started cleaning the dirt and paint off her body. I started with her face, since the thought of my hands anywhere near those incredible curves made me want to hit myself.

Slowly but surely, I was able to uncover the most beautiful face I had ever laid eyes on. She looked like she had been expertly crafted from my wildest dreams and coated in a thin layer of silver. Her skin was smooth, almost luminescent. And her eyes were fixed on me, drawing heat into my chest.

"What's your name?" I asked, unable to take the silence

anymore.

Without taking her eyes off me, she breathed deeply and let out a heavy sigh. Her chest caught my attention, and I mentally kicked myself again.

"Anjani," she finally answered. There was that voice again. Her perfect face showed absolutely no expression. She baffled me.

"Like I said, Jovi, stay sharp." Bijarki trashed my moment again. "We don't know what her allegiance is or what she's doing here."

"My allegiance is to my tribe and no one else!" Anjani shot back, her chin high and ego apparently bruised far worse than her gorgeous body.

Stop it.

"Where is your tribe?" I asked, determined to keep Bijarki's focus on treating her cuts and out of the conversation. He wasn't exactly a model of trustworthiness either. She focused her attention on me again, and my heartbeat moved into my throat.

I stole a glance at Phoenix. Serena was cleaning his head wound while Vita mixed some herbs and strangely colored liquids in a bowl, following the Druid's muttered instructions.

"My tribe is on the northern slope of the jungle mountain, a day's trip from here, more or less," Anjani replied, surprisingly calm and accurate. I turned my head back to look at her. Those eyes could capture my soul and hold it hostage for eternity.

"Whatever it is you think you're feeling, chances are it's not real." Bijarki's voice crashed down on my softened senses. "It's in our nature."

The woman scoffed and turned her head to the side, her eyes shut tight.

"Protest all you want, succubus," Bijarki growled at her, "but until you tell us what tribe you belong to and what you were doing around here, you're not to be trusted."

"I strongly recommend that you secure her arms and legs, just in case," Draven interjected from Phoenix's bedside.

"I'm Anjani, sister of the Red Tribe up north," she shot back, her husky voice tainted with pride. "We owe our allegiance to no one but ourselves! Azazel has not turned us!"

A long moment passed before Draven spoke again.

"As far as we know, almost all incubi have switched to his side, for the sake of survival rather than anything else," the Druid replied. "We don't know enough about the Red Tribe to simply take your word for it."

"Fine. Then tie me down. But when my sisters ask about my treatment here, I'll be sure to give them the full details," Anjani spat back.

Bijarki paused the treatment process and tied her wrists and ankles to the bed's iron frame with wide strips of linen.

She was met with silence. She looked uncomfortable and deeply offended, and I somehow wanted to make it better. I continued cleaning her skin, reaching down to her chest. She suddenly turned her head to face me.

"Go any lower, and I will tear your head off," she whispered, sending chills down my spine.

Bijarki noticed the tension as he applied the medicine on the last leg cut. "Jovi, what did I tell you—"

"I heard you the first time!" I snapped. I had zero patience left. I switched my focus to Anjani. "You can struggle and growl all you want, but the facts are obvious. You are hurt and filthy, and I can't let your wounds get infected from all this swamp dirt. I didn't risk my life and my friend isn't lying there unconscious for you to die on us because you're stubborn!"

I had mustered all my strength to project all of that in one fluid sentence. I even surprised myself.

Anjani's expression softened. She turned her head away, silently allowing me to continue wiping her down, one inch of perfect skin at a time.

I couldn't help taking all of her in—each curve, each line. Even the crimson paint and the patches of animal hide stretched over her breasts spoke of a fierce young woman, genetically engineered to seduce yet expertly trained to hunt and kill.

Bijarki left us for a brief moment to speak to Draven, but I registered the look he threw me over his shoulder. It was riddled with warnings.

I was well aware of the potential dangers, but I couldn't stop myself from wanting to see this incredible creature safe. The touch of her skin shot billions of electric signals through my fingertips.

The way she shifted on the bed made me realize that she was responsive to our contact. I just wasn't sure whether her response was one of discomfort or something else.

My head was heavy with guilt whenever I looked over at Phoenix, but every time I looked back at Anjani, my chest constricted, and my senses threw me for a loop.

Beautiful, but damn straight deadly.

SERENA
[HAZEL AND TEJUS'S DAUGHTER]

I swapped Field's shirt for a fresh towel dipped in water and applied pressure to Phoenix's head wound. My hands trembled, and my breath was ragged. A thousand thoughts raced through my mind as I watched the scene unfold before my eyes.

Vita followed Draven's instructions and retrieved a bundle of endemic herbs from a cabinet behind us. I was surprised by his calm demeanor and his accurate memory. Even blind, he still knew where everything was and what was needed to treat Phoenix's wound.

Across the room, Aida cleaned Field's cuts. Her face was flushed, her hair tousled, and her gestures rushed. Given her feelings for Field and the little faith that she had in herself when it came to him, I figured she was very uncomfortable being so close to him.

On the other side, Bijarki and Jovi looked after the wounded succubus. She looked our way occasionally, as if scanning us. I guessed she was trying to ascertain whether we were friends or foes. I was tempted to mind-meld with her to find out what her true intentions were and what she was doing near the house in the first place, but I had to save what little energy I had left to syphon pain from Phoenix.

I looked down at him. A slight frown drew his eyebrows closer. Bruises bloomed across his jaw in soft reds and violets, and his lower lip had cracked. I couldn't stand the sight of him hurt. It cut me to the core.

"Blend the red sage dust with water and let it sit for a minute," Draven instructed Vita.

I watched her obey him, her fingers shaking on the wooden bowl. She had never endured this much stress over the course of just a few days—none of us had. Since we weren't official GASP members yet, in The Shade, our biggest problems were fitting into dresses and picking out colleges to apply to. Our life back home seemed like a different lifetime now.

"Crush the roots and black seeds in another bowl and pour the red sage mixture over them," Draven continued almost mechanically. He leaned against the bedside for support.

Vita obeyed, and I watched as she mixed everything into a thick, dark red paste.

"What's that?" I asked.

"A proprietary blend we apply to open wounds. It's extremely effective." Draven softened his tone when speaking to me. I couldn't help but wonder whether it was out of pity or something else. I took a deep breath and heard my pulse drumming in my ears.

"What next?" Vita asked in a hushed, quivering voice. Draven's hand rested on her shoulder. She looked up at him and pursed her lips.

"First take a few deep breaths and relax your hands. I can hear how unsteady they are from the sound of you handling the bowl," Draven replied calmly.

Vita nodded and followed his advice. Draven's hand left her shoulder, passing through his ruffled hair before it settled on the side of the bed.

"Now you can apply that paste on his head wound," he continued. "Do it gently, and spread it around the wound as well. Once it dries up, it will stay there for a couple of days before it falls off by itself."

I removed my hands from the back of my brother's head, leaving room for Vita to work. I looked at her and felt an indescribable amount of affection and gratitude. Tears stung my eyes.

"Thank you, Vita. You're doing an incredible job. You've got this," I said, trying to reassure her. She smiled, nodded, and started applying the herbal mixture to Phoenix's head wound.

"I can't bear the thought of him in pain," I said almost to myself and placed my palms on his chest. I closed my eyes and syphoned whatever I could off my brother. I went deep into the darkness, searching for the colors of whatever he was feeling.

I looked for the familiar red of physical pain, but there was nothing there, just a disturbing pitch black. The silence worried me more than his wound.

I opened my eyes and inhaled, trying hard not to break down.

"I can't do anything," I said, breathing heavily. "There's nothing, just pitch black, like he's not feeling anything. Like he's dead."

"The blow to the head was most likely severe. I don't think his state has to do with pain but rather with unconsciousness. All we can do is wait for him to recover on his own," Draven replied.

His hand moved along the side of the bed until he found Phoenix's, and his fingers searched for his wrist. A few moments passed as Draven felt my brother's pulse.

"It's slow but steady," he concluded.

"What does that mean?" I asked. Tears escaped down my cheeks.

"It means he's stable but in a deep unconscious state. He'll need time to wake up."

"How much time?" I cried out, unable to control myself anymore. Vita looked up at me, concern darkening her turquoise eyes. She'd been holding everything in, and I realized that if I didn't regain my composure, she might crack as well. I needed her calm and focused while treating my brother.

I brushed away my tears hurriedly and tried to breathe in through my nose.

Draven waited for me to regain composure before replying.

"It could be a few hours or a few days," he said. "It all depends on his strength, and he strikes me as a warrior. I reckon he'll be back up and sprinting around in no time."

I had a feeling Draven said this more for my reassurance than as an actual fact, but I took it gladly. I didn't want to think about the darker alternatives.

I bent over to whisper in Phoenix's ear. I wasn't sure whether he could hear me, but I needed to speak to him. "Please stay strong. I need you now more than ever."

My chest constricted, and I swallowed another wave of tears. I straightened my back and took my brother's hand. I couldn't let go.

"What do we do now?" I asked Draven as Vita finished applying the herb mixture.

"As far as Phoenix is concerned, all we can do is wait," he replied. "I need to speak to Bijarki and figure out what our next steps will be. We have a stranger among us now, and we don't know what she wants. We can't trust anyone outside this group."

At the sound of his name, Bijarki turned his head to face us. His discreet nod indicated that he was determined to keep us all safe from the wounded succubus, even if she was one of his own kind. I couldn't help but find his nod reassuring.

I held my brother's limp hand. I couldn't deny that Draven's presence, so close to me, was also reassuring. To say that I genuinely admired him for his calm and steady demeanor in helping my brother—while I had been panicking and fumbling about—would have been an understatement.

"Thank you, Draven," I said quietly.

He set his jaw and nodded almost imperceptibly.

JOVI
[VICTORIA & BASTIEN'S SON]

A few hours went by, with Anjani drifting in and out of consciousness. The herbs Bijarki had applied on her wounds began to show their effects. Druid healing was an impressive thing to watch, as their combinations of natural elements worked faster than any human medication. It basically looked like magic.

I kept a close eye on the succubus, half of me unable to part from her while the other half stayed tense and wary. Her beauty was hypnotic, each line of her face seemingly designed to make a man fall to his knees and beg for her attention.

Her breathing had relaxed, and her chest moved in an even

rhythm, her silvery flesh pushing against the tight leather garments. My eyes wandered from her smooth jawline to her full breasts, her flat stomach, and her thighs. She could probably crush a man's ribcage with those legs.

Just as I was about to wonder what else she could do with her thighs, I felt my face burn. I looked to my right and found Anjani watching me. Once again, her expression said nothing, and that put me on my guard.

Several moments passed before her lips moved.

"Thank you," she whispered, and I instinctively nodded.

My fingers fumbled on the side of her bed, while I tried to think of something to say. I looked over at Phoenix, who was still unconscious. Serena sat on a stool by his side, holding his hand and talking to him.

"How are you feeling?" I asked Anjani. I was met with a shrug and figured I'd have to settle with just that.

But then I saw tears glazing her eyes. She gazed at the ceiling, biting her lower lip. I bit mine in response but kept my mouth shut.

"I'm better than my sisters for sure," she said. I thought back to her fallen companions.

"What happened in the jungle?" I asked.

"Strange things are happening all over the jungle," she replied. Her cryptic answer didn't satisfy my curiosity, but I didn't have the courage to drill for more information.

What is wrong with me?

I was supposed to be the strong one with Field and Phoenix down. I was responsible for protecting my sister and her friends. And yet I had little to no courage in front of this succubus. I mentally chastised myself for my weakness and pushed myself further.

"What do you mean?" I persisted.

Anjani took a deep breath before she replied. "The shape-shifters are much more brazen now. They used to only come out at night. Now, they roam the jungles in broad daylight, slashing at whatever crosses their path. And not just them. Other creatures have started coming out when they're least expected. We don't know why."

"What were you doing there, then?" Bijarki interjected, once again standing by the bed.

Anjani scoffed and turned her head to face me, scowling. She was making no effort to even be civil with Bijarki, though, to be fair, if I'd been wounded and tied to a bed by him, I wouldn't have liked him either.

"The more open you are with us, the quicker we can move this along," he said.

Anjani rolled her eyes while her arms struggled against her restraints. "Why should I trust you?" she snapped.

"Why shouldn't we just throw you back out into the swamp and let the shape-shifters finish the job?"

Anjani sighed. Resignation softened her demeanor. She relaxed again as she looked at me.

"I'm a sister of the Red Tribe. I've told you already. We're all succubi, but we barely mingle with our own kind. We stick to our little territory in the northern jungles, we hunt at night, and we keep our allegiance to ourselves," she said, her tone firm.

"What about Azazel? Has he not approached you?" Bijarki replied.

"He's sent out his Destroyers to meet with us, but we refused his terms and have kept them at bay ever since. We have no need for his filthy corruption." Anjani continued looking at me as she answered, as if willfully ignoring Bijarki's physical presence.

"How have you been keeping them at bay?" Bijarki narrowed his eyes and kept his focus on her. She shifted on the bed, and my hand instinctively reached out and touched her forearm. The second I did, the touch of her skin sent heatwaves through my body.

Anjani stilled and shot me a glare.

I removed my hand.

"We have our methods, incubus," she continued tersely, her chin high. "Don't worry. We'd rather die a thousand deaths before turning to his despicable side."

I wasn't sure if it was just me, but she seemed genuine and quite proud. I couldn't help but wonder what an entire tribe of warrior succubi like her could be like. Were they all as devastatingly gorgeous as she was?

"What about your companions?" I asked, following my train of thought. She turned her head to the side, avoiding both Bijarki and me.

"They were my sisters. We didn't know what we were getting ourselves into," she replied, her voice low and trembling.

"What were you doing around here?" Bijarki was relentless.

"I didn't know I was *here* until you grabbed me and ran away from the shape-shifters." Anjani frowned at me. I was embarrassed to admit it, but her continued, deliberate ignorance of Bijarki filled me with a sense of childish pride. "We had strayed too far south from our camp when the beasts ambushed us."

Five seconds of silence followed before Bijarki replied, "We'll have to verify your claims." He turned and left us.

I watched him stride back to Draven, probably to update him on what Anjani had told us. The suspicion was reasonable, even in my skewed opinion.

But she was on her own and had nearly died in that swamp. I didn't think anyone would pick a fight with a pack of shape-shifters just to get our attention. Outsiders couldn't see us or the mansion beneath the protective shield anyway.

I figured the only reason why she'd been able to pass the protective spell in the first place was because I had been holding her at the time, while the shape-shifters had knocked themselves against it, unable to go beyond. Maybe there were exceptions to the shield's rules, like we'd seen with Bijarki.

She was weakened and drowsy and clearly suffering over the loss of her sisters. Tears streamed down her cheeks. She closed her eyes and surrendered to the pain she'd kept to herself for the past few hours.

My hand moved toward her again and gently squeezed her arm in a humble attempt to comfort her.

This time she didn't object.

Vita
[GRACE AND LAWRENCE'S DAUGHTER]

It took all the strength I had to not collapse after I finished applying the herb mixture to Phoenix's head wound. I moved quietly, leaving Serena by her brother's side with Draven, and sought out the farthest corner of the room.

I found a little stool next to a medicine cabinet and sat down. My legs were jello and my breathing erratic. My pulse thundered in my ears. I closed my eyes for a few moments and tried to regain composure.

I looked over at Serena where she was sitting with her brother, then at Jovi and the succubus, and, before I could stop myself, over to Bijarki, who leaned against a spare bed, watching me. He was beautiful in all possible senses, like he'd been painstakingly drawn to achieve perfection. His broad shoulders were relaxed, his arms crossed over his chest. His military attire accentuated the sharp lines of his jaw.

His frown mirrored an emotion I couldn't really understand.

I realized my face was probably bright red and blotchy from all the stress and panic I'd just been through. It probably looked like I'd been crying, too, since my eyes felt glassy—I'd certainly come close to it.

The heat roasting the inside of my throat at the sight of the incubus was too much to handle in this moment. I hid my face in my palms and shut everything out. I focused on my breathing until it all seemed to go quiet around me.

Unnaturally quiet. The thought that I might be slipping into another vision crossed my mind, and I quickly opened my eyes. I really wasn't in the mood for another Oracle seizure right now.

I found Bijarki standing in front of me, looking down with a wet towel in his hand. He offered it to me. His face lacked any expression, but his bluish-gray eyes seemed to see right through me, making me feel vulnerable.

"You've got blood all over you," he said and gently pushed the towel into my hands.

I accepted it with a small nod and soon understood what he meant. Phoenix's blood was smeared all over my arms, and the realization made me shudder as I wiped it off. I had to scrub hard where the blood had dried and didn't come off easily.

I sighed and kept at it, aware of Bijarki still near me. I looked up, and my gaze met his for a second. He nodded respectfully and walked away. His presence had felt comforting.

He'd had a strange effect on me when we'd first met with my knees going weak all the time. I'd pushed all of that away, and I'd pushed him away as well, as he'd gotten too close too fast. I'd been closed off my whole life to guys. I didn't know how to react to him.

Even when I'd snapped at him, he'd been so respectful of my boundaries, almost leery of crossing paths again, yet he couldn't leave me on my own when he'd seen me suffering. In the beginning I had been wary and reserved around Bijarki, but those feelings had shifted to a strange but much-welcome calm whenever he was near me.

I wasn't sure what was happening to me, but, ironic as it was, I wanted him to turn around and stay a while longer.

SERENA
[HAZEL AND TEJUS'S DAUGHTER]

I lost track of time. I had dozed off on the stool next to Phoenix's bed for a while, my head resting against his side. When I came to, Aida and Field were standing nearby, both looking down at Phoenix with frowns of concern.

Aida gave me a pained smile. "How are you holding up?" she asked, her voice low.

I looked at my brother and saw that nothing had changed over the last few hours. He was still unconscious, but his forehead was smooth and gave me the impression that he was in a deep sleep, which was somewhat reassuring.

"I'm all right. Not sure about Phoenix." I sighed and rubbed my eyes.

Field was gently leaning against Aida, and she didn't squirm like I'd seen her do before when he was too close to her. At the same time, the look she gave me made me think that something had changed in their non-relationship. There was a mixture of childish giddiness, awe, and reserve passing over her face, in rapid succession, like she wasn't sure that it was all real. I guessed she was still processing how she felt about being in such close physical contact with him.

I wasn't sure whether he'd gotten closer or whether she'd gotten a bit more comfortable in his vicinity, but something was definitely different about them.

On any other day, I would've eagerly pulled her aside and interrogated the daylight out of her, but with Phoenix lying unconscious before me, I couldn't stay focused on Field and Aida.

I caressed my brother's face with the back of my hand, secretly hoping that he could feel me and wake up sooner. If he woke up at all.

I flicked the grim thought away as fast as I could and found myself wondering about Draven. I looked around and found him at the far side of the basement room by the stairs. He leaned against a wall, talking to Bijarki.

I couldn't do anything more to help Phoenix at this point in time, but I needed to focus on something. It made sense for me to resume my little mission to pump the Druid for information, especially with the succubus in our midst. There was a lot he still hadn't told me about the incubi and their female counterparts, their involvement with Azazel, and the risks they posed to our safety.

"Aida, can you look after Phoenix for a while?" I asked. "I need to talk to Draven."

"Sure, I'll stay with him." Her reply came swiftly, and I gave her the warmest smile I could muster.

"I'll stick around," Field interjected, still holding his side.

Aida threw him a look, and he shrugged with the expression of a little kid in trouble.

"You should be lying down in your bed," she said.

Field moved slowly around the bed and took my seat on the stool, grunting in the process. I felt so bad for him and the amount of pain he'd endured for my brother.

"I'm fine," he replied gently and looked up at me with a reassuring smile.

"I wish I could syphon some of that pain away, but I'm drained for now." I felt the need to explain myself.

"You've got to save your energy. Don't worry about me. Really." He waved me off, and I nodded.

I walked up to Draven, who was still in conversation with Bijarki. They both kept their voices low. My guess was that they didn't want the succubus to hear them. I looked over and saw her fast asleep, Jovi standing motionless by her bedside.

"What do we do next?" I asked Draven. He straightened at the sound of my voice. Bijarki, on the other hand, gave me a once-over and kept his mouth shut. We still didn't like each other very much.

"We need to keep this group safe. We're not sure of the succubus's intentions, regardless of what she tells us," Draven replied.

"What has she told us, exactly?" I still had no idea who she was.

"She calls herself Anjani of the Red Tribe," Bijarki answered.

I squinted at him, letting my short fuse show. I had very little patience for cryptic short sentences at this point.

"Is that supposed to mean anything to me?" I retorted.

Bijarki pursed his lips.

"The Red Tribe is only somewhat known in the north. They're all female warriors, with little to no contact with the rest of their species," Draven replied. "She says they've been resisting Azazel's Destroyers, but I have to see for myself." He sighed. "Or better yet, Bijarki will have to see for me."

I looked at Draven, then at Bijarki, whose gaze lowered to the ground. I wondered whether he was feeling sorry for the Druid or just pained by our shared handicap with Draven being visually impaired at such a dangerous time. I tried to drown out how guilty I felt, still bearing the responsibility of his blindness in my heart.

"So far she's been quiet and tied to the bed. I'm not sure she's much of a threat right now," I said.

"Nevertheless, her statements need to be verified. She said she strayed too far from her camp with her sisters when the shape-shifters attacked and that she didn't know about or see the mansion until Jovi brought her in," Draven said.

"How do you plan to verify anything she says?" I asked.

"The fire. Bijarki can look into it for me."

Bijarki stood silent next to him. I was under the impression that I intimidated him a little bit, judging by the way he avoided looking me in the eye and took a step back every time I came near him.

Good.

Draven's head cocked to one side, and my heart throbbed for a brief moment. "How are you feeling?"

I quickly dismissed his concern, as it didn't feel appropriate in the presence of the incubus. "I'm fine. I'm not the one who got hurt this morning. I'm the one who wants to do something about all of this. What about the sleeping Daughter?" I shifted quickly, hoping to catch him off guard.

"That's something we can discuss another time," he shot back, and I felt my resolve fizzle.

He placed his hand on Bijarki's shoulder and squeezed twice before they made to leave.

"Wait. Where are you going?" I shouted after them, irritation tainting my voice.

"I told you. The fire." His reply echoed from across the room.

I let out a long sigh as they left, and found myself without a plan. Draven didn't want me around while he had Bijarki for support, and that annoyed me a surprising amount. I couldn't sit by my brother's side either. My helplessness would scratch away at my soul, since I couldn't do anything more to help him. I had to find something else to do.

Maybe read more from Elissa's diary.

My gaze fell on Jovi and Anjani. I saved the thought of Elissa's diary for later that night, as I had doubts I'd be able to sleep. I walked over to get a closer look at the succubus.

She seemed submerged in a deep sleep. Her skin shimmered like Bijarki's, but there was something feral about her that I found troubling and fascinating at the same time. I had a feeling that the entire species would be able to make me feel that way— fascinated and scared simultaneously.

I watched her for a while, wondering about her, about how she'd come to cross paths with us, and about her intentions. Had she really just stumbled upon us in a desperate attempt to save her own life? Or had she been sent to infiltrate our group? A multitude of other questions flickered through my mind; some I had reasonable answers for, but others left me blank.

Jovi had cleaned her up well, and her wounds were covered

in one of the Druid's weird-smelling herbal remedies. He still stood by her side, his hands resting on her forearm and his gaze fixed on her face.

He had some scratches of his own but nothing as serious or as deep as Field or Phoenix or Anjani.

"You okay?" I asked him.

He looked at me, concern furrowing his brows. "I'm all right. How are you holding up? How's Phoenix?"

I shrugged, unable to think of a more eloquent gesture to explain how I felt. "Draven says it will take a while for him to wake up," I replied.

Jovi's heavy sigh rolled from his chest. He looked pained as he glanced at my brother lying in bed somewhere behind me. "This is all my fault, Serena. I am so sorry. I just couldn't let her get killed by those monsters."

It hadn't occurred to me to blame him. I would have done the same in Jovi's place; I would've done my best to save someone about to get torn to shreds by shape-shifters.

"Don't be stupid, Jovi. This isn't your fault," I replied.

A few moments passed as he digested my response. He glanced down at Anjani. I noticed the glimmer in his eyes, and I wondered about his attachment to the succubus, since he hadn't left her side.

"What is it with you and her?" I asked, perhaps a little more directly than I had intended.

His eyebrows rose in surprise. "What? What do you mean?"

"You're basically glued to a succubus. What's up with that?"

"I don't know what you're talking about," he replied, brushing me off.

But I didn't want to let it go just yet. If he was attracted to Anjani, it made him vulnerable and open to attacks, at least until her claims could be verified.

Jovi gazed at her, and his jaw tensed. Then he smirked at me.

"Don't be stupid," he said. "I'm just keeping an eye on her, making sure we're all safe."

"She's injured and tied to the bed, and you're hovering over her like a concerned nurse," I shot back. As if I'd ever buy his lame excuse.

"Nah, I'm literally keeping an eye on her," he insisted, then shrugged. "Besides, I'm the one who brought her here. She's kind of my responsibility."

I eyed him suspiciously, but decided to give it a rest. A headache snuck between my temples, and my knees felt weak. It had been a long day. I needed to sit down and process everything. I had to calculate my next steps carefully regarding Draven, and I had no energy left to focus on Jovi and his damsel in distress.

I nodded and took my leave. Time to read a few pages from Elissa's diary after all.

SERENA
[HAZEL AND TEJUS'S DAUGHTER]

There wasn't much left in Elissa's diary. The last entry was short and rushed, written in broken cursive and riddled with ink blots.

"*Almus has yet to return, and I have lost the ability to sleep in his absence.*

Draven asks me about him every day, and I am running out of excuses to ease his concerns. Poor little thing, so young yet so troubled with responsibilities.

I love him with all my heart. If it weren't for him, I would have lost my mind by now…

Another day has gone, and I'm once again here, on my own. The boy is fast asleep now, and I'm trying to keep myself busy with chores around the mansion.

I don't know what tomorrow will bring, but I hope it brings back the man I owe my life to—the man who has my heart."

I sighed as I put the diary away and headed for Draven's study. The reading session had been brief and unsatisfying and, at the same time, painfully revealing. There were no more entries by Elissa, which made me assume that something happened to her, that she was gone the next day.

I pushed open the door to Draven's study slowly, not wanting to barge in and startle him. I figured a blind man needed to be eased out of his solitude, contrary to my usual bull-in-a-china-shop demeanor.

The fire burned hot, and I instantly regretted my decision to seek him out. It was a sauna in there. But that wasn't the worst part. I found Draven furiously fumbling through the shelves on one of the walls. Books and various knick knacks kept falling on the floor while he cursed under his breath.

I watched him for a minute. What was he trying to do? Then I realized he was trying to find something. Judging by his muttered curses and grunts, he was failing miserably.

"Can I help you?" I asked.

Draven stilled, his hands on a shelf in front of him, and turned his head toward me.

"I'm downright useless right now. I can't take it anymore," he said.

"Well… I'm here to help. What do you need, Draven?"

He exhaled and allowed a moment to pass before he spoke again.

"I keep herbs in this room. Extremely rare specimens that I can ingest and that can help increase my other senses in the absence of sight," he said. "I have to make myself more useful. Time moves fast, and I can't keep up in this condition."

"Okay," I replied, my voice calm while my mind processed the information. This man was full of interesting secrets. I had to learn everything I could from him for as long as I was with him. "What am I looking for? Where do you want me to look?"

"There are three vials made of colored glass. I had them especially made for these herbs. One is a golden yellow, one is a dark pink, and the other is green. They're shaped like tears and are sealed with black corks."

"Do you remember where you put them?"

"They must be behind some books, somewhere on these shelves. I'm not sure which shelf, though. I've not seen them since I put them away a very long time ago." He leaned back against his desk.

I had to give him credit; for a blind man he was pretty quick at spacial recognition. He'd learned some of the key distances in his study already. It kind of made sense, since this was where he spent most of his time.

I went over to the shelves and started looking for the glass vials. As I fumbled between books, boxes, and various other items on the top side of the rack, I figured it was as good a time as any to resume my intel mission. I looked over my shoulder and watched him sink into the chair, quiet and still.

"Tell me more about Druids," I said. "I barely know anything about you."

"There's not that much to tell, really," he replied.

I sighed. I had a feeling he was in no mood to talk.

But then he continued. "We've been around for eons, ruling over the galaxy with a solid sense of democracy, like I've told you before. We're very close to nature." He paused, as if waiting for me to respond.

"Hence your penchant for herbs and mystic fires," I replied, my eyes focused on finding the vials.

"Indeed. We have a natural communion with the elements, with Eritopia itself. We respect life and everything it gives us. Druids are also dual creatures. We can morph into snakes."

I froze, then turned to gape at him. He'd been waiting for my reaction, his jaw firm and throbbing.

"You can turn into a *snake?*" Had I heard him correctly?

He nodded.

"Not much to tell my ass," I said in wonderment.

Everything started falling into place in my head. The blackness that had flickered over his eyes before the Daughters took his sight was the haw I'd seen on snakes, a membrane typical of reptiles. The heat in his study, his need to stay warm even with the scorching heat outside. The fact that I'd never seen him eat. It all made sense.

Wow.

It took me a minute to process it all. Part of me was curious to see him transform. But then another thought crossed my mind. I stilled.

"The Destroyers have snake tails," I said.

"Indeed, they do. They were all Druids once, just like Azazel," Draven explained. "Druid magic is deeply tied to Eritopia, to nature itself. But it can be as dual as our bodies are. It can be a natural art or a black art."

"What's the difference between the two?" I asked. I resumed looking for the vials. My fingers brushed over a leather bound copy of *Delirium: A Guide to Incubi Seduction.* I shivered a little, despite the heat, remembering Bijarki.

"We use plants and herbs and other natural ingredients to practice natural arts, and it's a clean process, mostly performed for healing, research, scrying, or even defense but never to attack or hurt anyone or anything. We draw energy from other creatures for the black arts, and it's a side of us I'm not willing to further elaborate on right now," Draven explained.

"And the Destroyers?"

"I'm getting there. In short, Azazel took the black art to a new, much darker, level skewing the process until he began corrupting Druids. Something festered inside of them, and they all began turning into snakes, unable to control the shift. By the time Azazel managed to get it under some kind of control, they were so irreparably damaged on the inside that they found themselves stuck halfway between Druid and snake."

The paintings made sense. The giant snake tails, the feral looks, their evil appearance—the Destroyers were the result of pure evil and greed corrupting the very soul of a Druid.

I returned to the million dollar question. "Tell me about the sleeping Daughter."

He immediately shifted in his chair and closed up on me.

I almost regretted asking, but he'd been dodging me on this for so long.

"Now isn't the time to talk about that." He tried to end the conversation there, but I wasn't ready to quit.

"Why are you so secretive about her? What are you afraid of?"

"Listen, Serena. I will answer any other question, except about her. She's the reason why we're protected here, and I will not do anything to endanger her just to satisfy your childish curiosity. I will protect her from us all, if that's what it takes to keep you safe. To keep the Oracles, your brother, your friends safe."

My breath hitched. "I appreciate that, Draven, but I think we're way past the stage of you not trusting me, or us for that matter. We've been through enough for you to give me a little credit here."

"Haven't you seen how cruel the Daughters can be? Do you think the sleeping one is any better? I don't want you anywhere near her." His tone was firm.

But I wasn't ready to give up just yet.

"I'm a big girl. I can handle myself. If she's our key to defeating Azazel, and since you're using my brother and my friends against him, I'm pretty sure I'm entitled to know a little bit more about the sleeping Daughter so I can be better prepared!"

Draven took a deep breath and ran a hand through his hair, a gesture I'd noticed he made whenever he was getting frustrated.

"You're not ready to understand more about her. This isn't about me not trusting you. This is about me trying to protect all of you and her at the same time. Me protecting her is what keeps you, all of you, *safe*. You don't fully understand what you're dealing with when it comes to the Daughters of Eritopia. Please, just let it go for tonight."

And there it was, a minor concession—for tonight. I scowled and allowed silence to fall between us.

"Please," he murmured, "just keep looking for the vials and help me get myself into better shape, so I can better protect you all." His voice was soft, his tone reserved.

I'd have to try and fight this fight again tomorrow, since he clearly wasn't going to reveal more now.

I reluctantly returned my focus to the task at hand. I rummaged through items I normally wouldn't have been allowed to touch, given how protective Draven was of everything in this room, but I eventually found them nestled behind a few herbology encyclopedias dressed in red leather.

"I found them," I said, clinking them in order to give him an audible glimpse of his cherished vials.

A smile bloomed on his face so radiant that I felt myself, and my annoyance with him, melt a little. Although maybe it was the fireplace melting me.

"What next?" I asked.

"I need you to mix them in a bowl. I'll have to eat them."

I pulled the cork off one of the vials and sniffed it. It smelled like twenty rotten corpses had been compressed into a tiny bottle, and it took everything I had to stop myself from heaving. I may have unwillingly gagged, because his smirk made me think he knew exactly what I'd done.

I followed his instructions and handed over the bowl with the stinky mixture. Why did the Druids' herbal magic have to smell so bad?

He took it and meticulously swallowed its content, one gulp at a time. The grimaces he made in between servings made me think that the smell was not the worst part of it. I gave him a glass of water to wash it all down.

Then I leaned against the desk, thinking about other ways to approach him tonight. The sleeping Daughter was out of the discussion for now, but I still needed him to open up some more. Maybe softening him up a little would work. He'd shown me his gentler side before, even if only briefly.

"Sorry if I'm being pushy, Draven," I spoke quietly, trying to infuse remorse into my tone. "It's just that with everything going on, with my brother downstairs, I need to think about something else. I need a distraction." I cautiously watched as his expression changed.

He pursed his lips and breathed out.

"Help me sit in my chair by the fireplace. I need the heat to speed up my metabolism and get the herbs absorbed into my system," he replied.

I nodded, forgetting momentarily that he couldn't see me, and helped him. Being so close to him again made my stomach churn as he leaned against me. He was heavy, but supporting him brought me a sense of satisfaction; his broad figure weighing against me made me feel like I was his anchor, that he relied on me, trusted me.

I sat him in his chair by the fire and seated myself on the floor next to him.

I gazed up at his stoic face. He had such a solid composure even when surrounded by chaos, even when everything in the world seemed to be going wrong. I realized that there was something about him that anchored me, too, despite his elusiveness. With my brother wounded downstairs and the prospect of Destroyers out to get us, Draven kept me on my toes and my mind away from dwelling on worst case scenarios that would have otherwise overwhelmed me.

I leaned my head against the wooden arm of his chair, careful not to touch him. I wasn't sure how aware he was of my proximity in this moment. We sat in silence for a while. I listened to the wood crackling in the fireplace and the sound of our slow breathing. A thousand other questions ran through my head, but they would have to wait. I'd clearly used up all my tokens for today.

Jovi
[Victoria & Bastien's son]

My legs gave out at some point during the afternoon. I sat down on the floor next to Anjani's bed, just to rest my eyes for a moment. I must have dozed off, despite the tornado of guilt and concern rattling me on the inside.

I opened my eyes and found myself looking at the ceiling. The once-white paint peeled off in curled crusts here and there. The dim light from the oil lamps gave everything a warm orange glow that melted into dark corners. It was quiet and, judging by how stiff my back and neck were, I must have been lying down for a couple of hours at least.

A flashback of Phoenix getting thrown to the ground by the

shape-shifters hit me, making my chest tighten. I took a deep breath. Despite Serena's reassurances, I still felt directly responsible for his condition.

Then I remembered why I'd done it. Anjani, the dangerously beautiful succubus who had almost become shape-shifter food. A burst of pride made me look up to catch a glimpse of the silvery damsel.

She looked down at me, leaning on her side. Whirlpools of gold and emerald lit her eyes, which grew large when they met mine. She quickly looked away and shifted on the bed to lie on her back. I guessed she hadn't wanted me to see she was looking. A smirk tugged at the corner of my mouth.

Maybe she's not made of stone after all.

I stood up and straightened my back. My bones crackled, and my muscles were uncomfortably sore, the result of the morning's strenuous activities.

I took a deep breath and felt my ribcage expand and relax. Soft scents of grass and spices flooded my nostrils, and I traced them back to Anjani. I'd caught her scent, and I had a hard time letting go.

But we still didn't know whether she was friend or foe. I mentally slapped myself and decided to try and engage in meaningful conversation.

"How are you feeling?" I asked.

That's the best you've got?

She looked away and said nothing.

"Do you need anything?"

I got the silent treatment and felt strangely offended. I'd just saved her life. The least she could do was give me some common courtesy. I'd earned it.

"You know, I don't deserve you treating me like this," I said.

She shot me an angry look, her lips tight and slim eyebrows frowning.

"I don't deserve being tied to the bed like a criminal either," she retorted, and it hit me that she felt offended by our suspicion. There wasn't much I could do to change that, at least not until the Druid and Bijarki confirmed that she was telling the truth.

I'd try lightening the mood instead.

"In all fairness, you can't tell me this is the first time a man has tied you to a bed," I quipped and followed up with my signature smirk, hoping to illicit at least a half-smile from her.

Anjani kept her face straight, but her beguiling eyes narrowed a touch. "Don't get ahead of yourself, boy. You would be physically unable to handle me."

I swallowed. Something told me she was right, and it stung.

Even worse, my cheeks heated, and my mind went blank. I had absolutely nothing to say in return, no way of soothing that burn. She was a whip.

Vita
[GRACE AND LAWRENCE'S DAUGHTER]

Later that night, I took my turn watching over Phoenix. I'd managed to steal an hour's worth of sleep upstairs, but the most recent vision of myself and Bijarki kept bothering me, replaying itself as a dream on a loop, making me wake up all heated up and sweaty.

One cold shower later, I was downstairs in the basement on a stool next to Phoenix. I'd checked his head wound; the herbal mixture stank less now that it was drying up. My heart tightened in my chest as I felt for his pulse. It was slow but steady. Nothing had changed in his condition. He was still deep under.

I saw his eyes move beneath their eyelids, a sign that he was most likely dreaming. It was an encouraging step forward, despite his overall unresponsiveness. At least there was brain activity. Maybe the herbs were doing a better job than I'd initially thought.

My mind went to Serena, wondering how she was holding up. Knowing her, I figured she'd stuck close to the Druid to keep herself distracted. She hated feeling useless.

I sighed and leaned against the wall behind me. It was cool and comforting at the same time. Aida slept in the bed previously occupied by Field. She was exhausted, and I couldn't blame her. She'd watched over Phoenix throughout the entire afternoon. She needed a break.

Field had gone out for a quick flight, just to give the surrounding area a once-over and make sure no other creatures were lurking in the darkness. It was a useless endeavor, I thought, since we were under the protective shield. But, then again, Field seemed to have made a habit of flying away every time he and Aida got too close, at least that was the pattern I'd noticed, anyway.

I'd glanced at them during the morning chaos. She'd been livid and soft at the same time, carefully cleaning his cuts while her cheeks were flushed and her fingers trembled uncontrollably. Despite the gravity of the situation, I couldn't help but smile. She probably never expected to end up so close to him.

But then Field's attitude had changed a little as well. I'd seen the way he looked at her while she struggled to keep her composure and treat his wounds. I wondered if Aida had noticed it as well.

I watched Phoenix's chest rise slowly with each breath, and my mind wandered. It inadvertently flew back to Bijarki holding me while I was half-asleep in his bed. The feel of his shimmering skin against mine. I was so soft and small, while he was nothing but strength and hard muscle. We fit perfectly against each other.

I remembered his breath on my neck, followed by fluttered kisses as he drifted in and out of sleep. Heat rose up to my temples.

Snap out of it!

I tried hard to think about something else, but I kept wondering why the future showed me and him at such a high degree of intimacy. How could we get so close when I'd repeatedly pushed him away, treating him like he was some kind of AMBER alert offender? Why would he still want me, after all the things I said to him the other day?

And there it was, the realization that it wasn't the vision of us getting together that baffled me. It was my own insecurity creeping up to the surface, that question of why he would want to be with me anyway.

The more I thought about what the future seemed to hold for me and Bijarki, the more confused I became. Did I want him? Was I developing feelings for him? Was I okay with the prospect of intimacy between us?

I took another deep breath, shoving the entire idea to the back of my head. I had a long night ahead of me, and I had a responsibility to look after Phoenix. It was pretty much the only thing I could do to avoid thinking about my fate as an Oracle, about Azazel and his Destroyers, about Bijarki, and about everything else that was wrong in this world.

I noticed Jovi get up from the floor and exchange a few words with Anjani. She was still tied to the bed and didn't seem comfortable. I felt sorry for her. She'd been viciously attacked and nearly killed by shape-shifters, lost her sisters, and had wound up tied to a bed in a Druid's basement. But, until we knew for sure that she was telling the truth, we couldn't risk having her roam the mansion freely.

Not after all the horrible things I'd seen were coming.

I watched Jovi's playful smirk leave his face. I couldn't hear what they were saying, but judging by his expression, he'd most likely said something stupid, and Anjani had shot him down.

His playful behavior and ability to take everything in stride were endearing. I didn't want him to change.

I didn't want him to die.

My mind returned once again to the terrifying vision of my cousin being impaled by a spear.

How can I stop it all from happening?

SERENA
[HAZEL AND TEJUS'S DAUGHTER]

"Serena, wake up." Draven's voice rumbled through my dreams.

It was well past midnight when I woke up. My lips were dry, my throat was parched, and my back hurt like a thousand knives had been jammed into it—the perks of falling asleep on the floor in front of a fireplace in the middle of a hot summer day. Druids be damned.

I slowly got up, adjusting my eyes to the dim, yellow light. I straightened my back and moved my head around in an attempt to relieve some of the tension that had gathered in the back of my neck.

I'm so thirsty.

I looked up to find Draven sitting in his chair. The fire threw shadows across his face. I had a prime view of his profile from my new angle. The blade of his nose stood out, reminding me of relief sculptures from Ancient Greece. I had to give him credit; for all his faults, Draven was one of the most beautiful creatures I had ever laid eyes on.

He was still and quiet, and I wondered whether I'd just dreamed him calling out to me.

"Did you say something?" I asked and rubbed my eyes. I passed my hands through my hair. It felt heavy and tangled. A bath was very much needed, especially after all the involuntary sweating during my snooze-fest by the fire.

"I said, 'wake up,'" he replied. "Glad to see you listened to me for once."

"Hey, that's not fair." I got up. There was some water left in a jug on his desk, and I gulped it all down without bothering to get a glass. The liquid was room temperature, but it still soothed my parched throat.

"You're right. I was being unnecessarily mean. You've come a long way since you first got here." A smirk quirked the corners of his mouth.

"How are you feeling?" I asked, wondering whether his super secret special herbs had done something or not.

"Still blind," he quipped.

I had no response to that. A moment of awkward silence

passed before he spoke again.

"But the herbs are working rather well," he said.

"What do you mean?"

I leaned against the desk, my legs still weak and half-asleep. It had been an excruciatingly long day.

"My other senses are heightened. I can hear your heartbeat, for example," he replied, his voice low and wavering. "Ba-boom... Ba-boom... Ba-boom..."

I put a hand on my chest and found that he'd perfectly captured the rhythm of my heartbeat. It was a very intimate observation, I thought, and I felt my heart pump faster.

"Now it's beating faster," he noticed. "Have I upset you?"

I shook my head and took a deep breath, willing myself into control. His accuracy was alarming, and it made me feel defenseless in front of him. Even vulnerable.

"No, not at all. I was just testing your hearing," I retorted.

He smiled again. "I can hear all the hearts beating in the house," he said. "Vita is awake in the basement. Phoenix is still asleep but stable and steady. Aida is sleeping. Bijarki, Jovi, and the succubus are also downstairs. Field is outside. I can't hear him."

I was officially impressed.

"Wow. What else can you do now?"

Draven cocked his head to the side, and his nostrils flared. "Did you know we all have our own individual scents?" he asked softly.

I waited for him to continue, unsure of where this was going.

"Like chemical reactions deep within our layers of skin, specific aromas that define us as individuals."

"I've never really considered that," I said.

"Well, we do. We all smell different, but with a little bit of practice, a Druid such as myself can use his amplified olfactory sense to identify a person based solely on their natural scent."

I had an idea as to what he was about to say. Unsurprisingly, my body immediately responded by flaring up, flooding my limbs with liquid heat.

"You, for example. You smell like summer by the sea. I've only been that far out once, years ago, but I remember it to this day. Driftwood and a subtle layer of blossoming lilies. That's you, Serena," Draven continued, his tone low as the amber light from the fireplace danced on his jaw.

I had nothing to say to that. I felt naked, raw, and like I was his to play with. I'd never taken my own scent into consideration. I'd never smelled myself to recognize what he described as being the proprietary fragrance of my skin. It was such an intimate thing to say. It went far deeper than his interpretation of my heartbeat.

My knees weakened, and I could feel my breathing staggering. But leave it to Draven to ruin the moment.

"There's a plethora of scents coming from downstairs as

well," he continued matter-of-factly. "Jovi and Aida share a common whiff of wet dog, but it's extremely subtle. She's more towards a bergamot, while Jovi leans into prairie grass and morning dew. Vita is a little fireball, soft layers of spices. I could go on, if you'd like." He smirked.

"No, no, I'm good. You lost me at wet dog anyway." My reply was blunt and followed by a sigh.

It felt good to see his spirits higher than before. He'd hated feeling useless, being unable to do everything he was used to doing. Until the Daughters returned his eyesight, Draven had to find other ways to stay active and protect us from Azazel and the Destroyers. I understood his frustration, but I was unable to fully understand his impairment. So it warmed me to see him cracking bad jokes and exploring his heightened senses to such impressive levels of detail.

My train of thought derailed completely as he stood up.

I rushed to offer my shoulder for support, but he raised his hand to stop me.

"Don't. I'm adjusting to spacial perception now. Sounds, smells, vibrations—they're telling me where everything is around me." He took a few steps.

I felt the need to remind him of my usefulness. "I'm right here if you need me." I was still on a mission to unlock all the mysteries that made Draven who he was. The more I learned from him, the better my friends, my brother, and I could defend ourselves against everything that wanted us dead in Eritopia. I hadn't forgotten about the last Daughter, either.

Draven walked toward the door, and his hand reached the doorknob without hesitation. Before opening the door, he turned his head to me.

"I'm not sure I should move around by myself. It might take a while for me to adjust to my surroundings. This is all quite new to me. I've never experienced the world in such detail without my eyesight." His honesty disarmed me and jolted me into action.

I moved to walk next to him, and his hand rested on my shoulder again. I was so used to this by now—it felt right. It felt natural.

We walked slowly toward the basement stairs, and I was impressed by his unwavering stance. He didn't need me for guidance. His steps were firm, and his direction was accurate and determined. Nevertheless, I kept myself at his side as we reached the basement room.

Phoenix was still unconscious, as I'd expected, with Jovi watching over him. Vita lay in a spare bed, as did Aida, while Bijarki stood by Anjani's bed. His gaze lit up when it found us at the bottom of the stairs. We reached him swiftly to find the succubus still tied to the iron frame, as beautiful as ever.

"We need to talk, Anjani." Draven addressed the succubus, who shot him an irritated look, not bothered by the bandage on his eyes.

She sighed.

"Bijarki and I found your tribe. We know where they are. We've seen some of your other sisters keeping watch over the camp," he said, and Bijarki nodded in confirmation.

I figured Draven had made Bijarki peer through the same fire I'd seen our families through. A pain of longing shuffled through me, but I tucked it away.

"You said you would 'verify my claims.' How'd that go?" Anjani sneered as she quoted Draven. Despite her feral demeanor and unknown intentions, I kind of liked her.

Both Bijarki and Draven paused for a moment.

"Point is, we are safe because nobody knows we are here, particularly Azazel. So, you should be able to understand why we don't take kindly to strangers," Draven said.

"It's not like I planned to be here in the first place. Your friend over there decided to stick his nose where it didn't belong and bring me here." Anjani nodded toward Jovi, who instantly straightened his back with indignation.

"Hey, I saved your life!" he shot back.

Anjani took a deep breath, closing her eyes for a brief moment.

"*Det'chalani.*" She spoke in what I assumed was some ancient tongue. Bijarki shifted his weight from one foot to the other, interest sparked.

"Right!" he concluded, knowing what she'd meant. We, on the other hand, didn't.

"Care to elaborate?" I asked.

"It means life debt," Bijarki explained, and Draven nodded. I could almost hear a plan hatching in his head, judging by the look on his face. "We saved her life, so she is in our debt. It's an ancient custom of our kind, extremely valuable and sacred."

"I owe you a life debt," Anjani continued, her voice low. "I owe your friend over there a life debt, to be precise." She nodded toward Jovi again, who glanced at us from my brother's bedside.

"Indeed you do," Draven concluded. "What are you proposing?"

A few moments passed before the succubus spoke again. "Whatever you need and I can do without putting my life at risk, I will do for you," she answered.

"Can you take us to your tribe, then?" Draven asked quickly. I had a feeling he'd had that question locked and loaded, just in case.

Anjani pondered the idea, then nodded.

"Since your tribe is one of the very few left resisting Azazel, we could forge an alliance and increase all our chances against his expansion," Draven continued.

"You'll have to bring something to the table. My sisters will not respond to reckless or suicidal plans against a throng of Destroyers," Anjani replied.

"Worry not, we have interesting tricks up our sleeves," Draven said with a satisfied smirk. I guessed he meant my brother, Vita, and Aida. The Oracles were crucial in a successful strategy against a power-hungry monster like Azazel. On top of that, my mind also wandered to the sleeping Daughter. Perhaps she was one of the tricks he'd mentioned.

I frowned at the thought of my brother and friends being considered pawns in a war against an evil warlord. But as more time passed, it was also becoming clear that war might be our only option if we ever wanted to get back home.

"I'll travel with her tomorrow to arrange a meeting with their tribe chief," Bijarki said, pulling me back into the present.

"I'm coming as well," Draven replied.

Wait, what?

"What do you mean you're coming as well?" I blurted. "You're severely incapacitated, even with your magical herbs and super-sharp senses, where do you think you're going?"

Draven shook his head, and his hand left my shoulder, seeking Bijarki's for support instead.

Irritation flashed through me.

"I'm perfectly capable of anything I set out to accomplish, including a visit to a neighboring tribe," he said. "Besides, I need to speak to the tribe, since I'm not sure they'll like Bijarki much on his own." He grinned.

I looked at the incubus, who was visibly annoyed, rolling his eyes and pursing his lips.

"What do you mean?" I asked.

"We do not take kindly to the males of our species," Anjani smirked from her bed. "We have very little respect for them."

"Oh, I see," I murmured, nodding. Then I remembered Draven's insane idea. "You're insane if you think I'll let you wander off into the jungle like the blind bat that you are right now!" A range of emotions overwhelmed me from anger to frustration to helplessness. He showed little regard for his own safety in his spur-of-the-moment decisions.

"I'm going with Bijarki and Anjani. I won't be on my own," Draven replied. "While I appreciate your concern, it's unnecessary."

Wow.

I wanted to say more, but the tension in his jaw made me realize I had just disrespected him in front of a stranger. The succubus watched us with renewed interest, the shadow of a smile on her lips.

"Bijarki, I need you to prepare everything we need for our travel tomorrow." Draven addressed the incubus, ignoring me.

Bijarki nodded with a frown. He didn't seem too happy about the arrangement either, but, unlike me, he didn't object. Instead, he and Draven turned to leave.

"Wait," Anjani interjected. "What about me?"

"What about you?" Bijarki shot back.

Anjani shook her restrained arms and flinched from the shoulder pain. She'd probably forgotten about the wound.

"Oh, that. We'll set you free in the morning when we leave," Draven replied and left, following Bijarki's lead up the stairs.

Anjani struggled against the bed, growling and hissing and cursing in words I didn't understand, before she resigned herself and let out a long, painful sigh. I was left standing next to her, lacking purpose or any idea of how to sneak myself back into the Druid's good graces.

How was I supposed to know he'd be so sensitive?

Guilt crept up on me. I had been too abrupt and loose with my words, calling him a blind bat and snapping at him the way I had. But he did have a habit of causing me to blow my lid.

Me and my stupid mouth.

SERENA
[HAZEL AND TEJUS'S DAUGHTER]

I was the first one in the basement to wake up in the morning. I'd sent Aida and Vita upstairs to sleep in the relative comfort of our bedroom. Jovi stayed to watch over Anjani. I'd pulled one of the spare beds closer to Phoenix's and spent some time trying to fall asleep, lying on my side and watching my brother.

Once I managed to drift off, my dreams were a mixture of horrors and wonders. Draven was deeply embedded in my subconscious. I kept seeing him talking to me and smiling at me, which made me feel good, even happy. But then the poisoned spears of Destroyers shot through the moving picture of him, and I witnessed my brother and my friends get tied down and thrown into rusty old cages. I saw the same sequences over and over, and each time their violent ending threw me back into consciousness with a jolt.

To say that I'd had a difficult night would have been an understatement. I sat up and stretched, still sore from my nap on the floor in Draven's study. I looked over to find Anjani in deep sleep. Jovi had pulled another spare bed next to her sometime during the night and was snoozing on his belly.

I stood up and moved to my brother's side. He was still unresponsive, but his breathing was even. I caressed his cheek with the back of my hand, just enough to get a feel for his temperature. He seemed okay, not too warm or too cold.

Last night's abrupt ending and Draven walking out with Bijarki and leaving me behind rushed back into focus. They were going to take Anjani back to her tribe, while I was stuck here, hoping they survived the trip and returned in one piece.

I pursed my lips. *No, no, no. He's not going anywhere without me.*

I didn't fight that thought, mainly because I had to keep myself close to Draven and uncover all the secrets he kept beneath that brooding mask of his. I looked down at my brother and chewed my lower lip.

I'd have to leave Phoenix here. I was of no use to him anyway. All he had to do was wake up and be okay. Aida and Vita would be around for him. He'd be safe, while Draven would soon be out in the open with who knew what other dangerous creatures lurking in that jungle.

I went upstairs, mentally preparing myself to resist Draven's impending opposition to my joining the expedition. Knowing him, there was no way he'd let me come without a fight. I didn't have much of a choice either, since his Royal Stubbornness was dead set on reaching out to a tribe of warrior succubi he knew very little about.

I reached Draven's bedroom upstairs and didn't bother to knock. I found him sitting up in his bed, his muscular chest and broad shoulders bathed in the morning light. The runes on his skin had faded substantially, now mere shadows the color of burnt coffee. He turned his head toward me.

"I could hear your heartbeat rushing up the stairs, but there was no way I'd be able to make myself decent in the time it took you to get here," Draven said with a half-smile.

"It's not like I haven't seen your bare chest before," I quipped and mentally prepared myself to inform him of my decision to join him on the trip.

But then I stilled, watching as he moved his head around slowly. He parted his lips. The tip of his tongue gently passed over his upper teeth, and heat burst at my very core. The image of him half-naked and licking his lips deleted my thoughts entirely. I was unable to move, my eyes fixated on his pink tongue sliding along his upper lip.

My stomach churned, and I wondered whether he was aware of what he was doing, of his effect on me. It struck me as particularly brazen given his usual reserve toward me, which baffled me even more. Until he spoke.

"The weather's good for travel today," he said.

What?

I was confused.

He got out of bed, shortening the distance between us.

"How do you know?" I asked, trying to get my breathing under control and my eyes off his lips.

Draven cocked his head to one side and whipped out an all-knowing smirk.

"I can feel it on my tongue," he replied, and it occurred to me that snakes used their tongues for smell, picking up the tiny moisture particles in the air. The Druid on magic herbs was a supercharged Druid and thus able to fully use his serpent abilities while not in snake form.

Embarrassment poured over me like a bucket of hot water, burning my cheeks and making me cringe, as I realized I had confused his tongue flicking for a sexual gesture.

I quickly remembered my purpose for coming to see him in the first place.

"I'm coming with you today," I declared, my chin high and steel threaded into my resolve.

A moment passed before he replied. "Out of the question."

"Nope, I am coming with you. There's no way I'm letting you go by yourself." My determination echoed in my voice.

"You're not leaving the mansion. The shield is the only thing keeping you alive right now."

"No, I'm keeping myself alive. Stop underestimating me," I shot back and took a step forward.

"Serena, you're not coming. I can't risk you getting hurt. There are shape-shifters and all kinds of other equally deadly creatures in the jungle," Draven replied. He took a step toward me, shrinking the distance between us. My heart pumped voraciously in my chest, and I tried hard to control it, all-too aware that he could hear it.

I tried to reason with him instead. "You're about to go see a tribe of warrior succubi you know very little about. I don't know about you, but I'm not comfortable with that thought."

He raked a hand through his hair, a sign that he was wavering just a little bit. He thought it over for a second, then put on his typical smirk. "Worried they'll try to seduce me?"

His blood-boiling arrogance was his weapon of choice for distracting me. Unfortunately for him, I was much better equipped to force him into submission.

"Don't be a jerk! They could kill you on sight!" I retorted.

"No."

"Draven, I am coming with you, whether you like it or not. You might find my sentry abilities useful. I might even save your ass for once, if push comes to shove!"

"No."

"Keep saying no, if it makes you feel like you're in charge, but I am coming with you. If you leave without me, I will follow you. There's no way I'm not coming. Get that through your thick, Druid head."

I exhaled and took another step forward. He towered over me, his face inches from mine. I held my breath, while he licked his lower lip, then bit it.

The silence weighed heavy between us, while I prepared my last blow.

"I'm not letting you go without me."

"Serena…"

His shoulders dropped as he exhaled his defeat. "Fine," he said. "Fine."

I grinned with tremendous satisfaction but couldn't take my eyes off his face. His jaw was clenched, the muscle throbbing.

"I really can't put up with your stubbornness this early in the morning," Draven added, irritation dripping from his voice.

I wasn't fazed. I'd won. It felt too good.

"I need to get dressed," he said.

"I'll help," I automatically said and fetched a shirt from his dresser.

He stood in the middle of the room, motionless, as I took his hand and placed the white linen garment in it. His fingers clutched it for a brief moment, then he moved to put it on.

I watched quietly as his arms stretched, one at a time, to sink into the sleeves. His muscles extended and vanished beneath the fabric. One button at a time, his torso was comfortably hugged by the shirt, his fingers meticulous and patient.

I pulled a dark chestnut coat from the dresser and gave it to Draven to put on. Not that I was an expert in 1800s fashion, but I couldn't help but gawk at the sight of him and the way the layers of velvet and linen wrapped around his body and further amplified his tall figure.

He sat back on the bed and asked for his boots, which I handed over from the side of the bed. He pulled the thick leather Wellingtons up.

I opened my mouth to ask him about the Daughter again. After all, I'd already defeated him once in a game of wills.

"Don't even bother asking me about the Daughter again," he said. "I'm really not in the mood for another history lesson right now."

I pouted, wondering if I really was that predictable.

"How did you—"

"I'm getting to know you better than you think, Serena," he interjected, his voice soft and deep. He stood up. "I'm well aware of your interest in the matter, and I will endeavor to tell you more once we reach the Red Tribe. I'm just kindly asking that you have some patience with me."

I nodded. It made sense, and we'd made great progress since our first day here. He was beginning to open up, but he was doing it in his own rhythm, bending his own rules in the process. I decided to give him some space on the issue until we reached the tribe. I secretly made a note to nevertheless try sneaking a question on the way there, just to see if I could.

"Okay," I conceded.

He reached forward, placing his hand on my shoulder. "I've lived most of my life in isolation. Then you crashed into it, and I'm still wrapping my head around you, adjusting as best as I can." Draven smiled and squeezed my shoulder, signaling me to move.

His words poked me in the chest. I cleared my throat and headed for the door.

We had a long journey ahead of us.

Vita

[Grace and Lawrence's daughter]

Serena took her turn watching over Phoenix after midnight, and I went upstairs and collapsed onto our bed. It took me forever to fall asleep. My mind kept dwelling on Bijarki. And when I finally did drop off, even in my dreams, I couldn't escape him. I wasn't sure whether I'd had more visions of the future in my sleep or if my brain was just playing fast and loose with the visions I'd already had of him, but the array of scenes that flickered before my eyes was intense.

When I woke up the next morning, it was to bright sunshine and Aida sound asleep next to me. I was flushed and hot, beads of sweat lining my eyebrows. I wiped them off with the back of my hand and breathed in the cool morning air, going over the few dream fragments that I still remembered.

An enormous canopy bed in the middle of a poppy field. Soft white sheets of translucent fabric undulating with the wind. The sky, enormous and blue above. And me and Bijarki sitting in the middle of the bed looking at each other. His fingers touched my face, then moved slowly down my neck, tracing the contour of my shoulder all the way to my wrist before he took my hand in his and pulled me into his arms. He whispered something in my ear, but I couldn't remember what he said. I only remembered how my heart fluttered at the sound of his low, husky voice. We melted in a long kiss, his lips over mine in a perfect fit…

The sound of snakes hissing pulled me back to consciousness.

No wonder I was feeling hot and flustered.

But I quickly shifted from flushed to irritated, remembering what Bijarki's special ability was as an incubus.

He wouldn't dare.

I narrowed my eyes as I got out of bed and padded to the window. Lo and behold, he shimmered in the sunlight, wearing his military suit as he brought out a couple of duffel bags from the house and placed them by one of the magnolia trees out front.

Would he?

My blood simmered as I saw him look up and notice me at the window.

He stilled, his cool eyes fixated on me. I could almost feel him drilling into my soul, but I wasn't sure whether it was his nature or just my reaction to his presence, even at this distance. My knees quivered.

I clutched my fists at my sides and rushed downstairs. I had to confront him. I had to find out whether he'd been playing his incubus tricks on my mind while I slept. I needed a reason for those intense and colorful dreams of him touching me in ways I'd never been touched before. My cheeks burned.

I darted through the mangled foyer, jumping over the wooden threshold, the only part of the doorway left intact after yesterday's emergency landing. Someone had swept away all the broken glass.

Bijarki stood by the magnolia tree where I'd last seen him, looking into the distance.

I allowed the anger of his potential invasion of my mind to engulf me. I needed all the rage I could possibly muster to confront him and call out his underhanded tactic. It must have been his fault. He must have manipulated my dreams.

"Hey, you!" I called out as I marched across the front lawn. The grass was soft and still dressed in morning dew, reminding me that I was barefoot. Despite the sunny sky, the temperature outside wasn't that hot, and I felt chills running down my spine and arms.

He turned to face me, and his blank expression faltered my

step. He scanned me from head to toe, and his eyes darkened as they reached my torso. The light breeze blowing through my nightgown made me aware that I was only wearing a flimsy, semi-transparent organza nightgown I'd found in the attic the other day. It may have been long and covering me from neck to toes, but the fabric was as thin as they came, in soft shades of pale green.

Bijarki had a pretty good view of my body beneath the gown, as I strutted toward him, struggling to hold on to the anger before embarrassment snuck up on me. His eyes flitted over my breasts as I closed the distance between us and poked him in the chest with my index finger.

"Have you been playing tricks on me in my sleep?" I demanded.

Deep blue and silver mingled in his eyes, as he lifted them to meet mine. "What are you talking about?" His gruff voice shot tiny sparks through my veins.

"Have you been manipulating my dreams? Dropping thoughts, bending my mind in my sleep or whatever it is you incubi like to do to women?" I was surprised I still had so much energy in my voice. His gaze captured mine and refused to let go, while I struggled to stand straight before him.

The breeze grew stronger for a fleeting moment, enough to blow through my nightgown and flutter the organza against my body. Bijarki's eyes dropped again to my thin nightgown, breaking the stare.

"I would never," he said slowly, his eyes wandering along the pale green fabric.

I had a hard time finding my next words.

"Vita, I swear on everything I hold dear in this world that I would never invade your dreams or push your will in any way," he continued. "I don't want you to do or feel anything that isn't yours to feel. I respect you too much."

My frustration bubbled beneath the quiet surface, but I couldn't deny the truth I saw in his gaze. Reluctantly, I concluded that he was being honest. The dreams weren't his doing. They were mine and mine alone. My heart pounded in my chest, and I swallowed, unable to say anything in return.

Shame and embarrassment crept up and burned my throat. I looked away, trying to focus on something in the distance—a tree, a shrub, anything that I could focus on to regain my composure.

Bijarki didn't move, and he didn't take his eyes off me; I felt them searing into me.

"What is it you think I made you dream of?" came the question I didn't want him asking.

I couldn't bear to look at him, but I sensed he was smiling through his words. "It's nothing important," I replied, my voice barely a whisper.

"It must have been, since you felt the need to walk straight out of bed to confront me about it." He wasn't ready to let this go.

I looked at him and instantly regretted it, as his gaze once again captured my breath.

"It doesn't matter. It wasn't you, and I apologize for wrongfully accusing you." I tried to keep myself upright, waging an internal battle against my jello legs.

He tilted his head to one side, and his expression softened to one that made my blood rush all over, prickling my fingers and toes. "Did you dream about me, Vita?"

"It's none of your business," I said and turned my back on him. I couldn't bear another minute so close to him. His proximity had a devastating effect on my self-control, and I needed time and space to process that, to accept that all these hot dreams I'd been having of Bijarki were the product of my own desires.

He didn't insist. "My apologies," he replied. "But I will continue to keep my distance, as per your request. I'm going away, so you won't see me for a few days anyway. It should bring you some comfort."

I froze. Fair enough. It should have brought me at least some form of relief. But the part of me that had been eager to be near him was thoroughly disappointed.

I turned my head just enough to get a glimpse of him from the corner of my eye. "How so?" I asked, hoping I sounded as disinterested as I intended.

"Draven and I are taking Anjani back to her tribe. We're looking to forge an alliance with the succubi against Azazel and increase our chances at fighting back."

I nodded, but all I could think of was an entire tribe of succubi as shimmering and seductive as Anjani surrounding Bijarki under the moonlight, their hands moving down his body, fingers delighted by his silvery skin. I shifted my weight from one leg to the other, trying to move past the uncomfortable state I'd put myself in.

I'd come at Bijarki so strong and aggressive and horribly wrong about his intentions, and he was about to go meet with an entire group of devastatingly gorgeous succubi, leaving me on my own with my frustrations and shame. I couldn't bring myself to talk about this with anyone. How had my most intimate thoughts and dreams become so tangled with my visions of the future?

My transition as an Oracle seemed to be just as eventful as Aida's, except mine played different mind tricks, making me confuse real visions and lustful dreams of Bijarki. Like I didn't have enough to deal with already.

The silence weighed heavily between us. He waited for me to respond, but when I didn't say anything, he turned to the mansion.

He passed me, throwing me a fleeting look that I couldn't

decipher—a sideways glance with his silver-blue irises flaring at me—and walked toward the main entrance with broad steps.

"Bijarki," I called out, this time in a softer tone.

He stopped and looked over his shoulder.

"Please be careful," I said. "Come back in one piece."

Bijarki turned to face me, and I held my breath. Thoughts seemed to run through his mind as his eyebrows slightly twitched. He opened his mouth as if to say something, but nothing came out.

I didn't have much to offer in order to make up for my earlier blunder, but at least I could be a decent person and try not to make him feel like I loathed him. "We're all safer with you around, whether we like each other or not," I added, just to make sure I was getting the right message across.

His face lit up, and he nodded, turned, and disappeared into the mansion.

A few days with him absent would be a good thing. It would provide me with an opportunity to reflect on everything and put things in perspective. I needed to understand how I felt about him and to figure out what, if anything, I could do about it.

JOVI
[Victoria & Bastien's son]

I slept like a rock. Not a single dream, just deep slumber away from everyone and everything. The previous day's events had obviously sucked my energy dry. When I awoke, Anjani was gone. I didn't see Serena or the Druid anywhere, and then I remembered they'd talked about traveling up north to meet with her tribe.

I glanced to my right to find Phoenix still comatose. As I watched his chest rise slowly with each breath, I felt guilty. I'd only been trying to do the right thing by diving into the jungle yesterday, but nothing could change the fact that, if I hadn't done it, Phoenix wouldn't have left the boundary either. He wouldn't be in this condition now.

I sat up and threw my legs over the side of the bed. A shower would do me wonders.

About twenty minutes later, I emerged from the bathroom fresh and ready. To do what exactly, I didn't know. But I couldn't sit still.

I went to one of the windows and pulled the dusty curtains aside. The sun inundated the room. I looked outside.

Draven and Serena were in the garden out front, standing next to a couple of duffel bags and talking. Serena pointed at the house. Out came Bijarki with Anjani leaning against him for support. He had one arm wrapped around her waist, helping her walk, and the other he used to hold what looked like a couple of short crossbows.

I didn't like that image.

I didn't like staying in the mansion while they were out trekking through the jungle either.

"No way I'm getting left behind," I growled beneath my breath. I grabbed my coat and rushed downstairs.

I went outside and found the four of them congregating around the duffel bags. Serena held one of the crossbows, looking at it with interest. Anjani had a leather quiver filled with short arrows. Their brightly colored feather ends drew my attention.

"What's going on here?" I asked as I reached the group.

Anjani didn't bother to look at me, keeping her eyes fixed on the quiver.

"We're getting ready to go out," Bijarki answered.

Serena kept turning the crossbow over to get a better look at the details. "This looks really cool," she said with a smile.

I'd forgotten about her fascination with ancient weaponry. Serena used to come with Aida and me when our parents took us to war museums in the human world. It was one of the few combat-related passions that she'd shared with Aida since they were little. I found it endearing that she still marveled at this kind of stuff.

"Crossbows, huh?" I quipped.

"Yeah, Anjani's taught us some nifty tricks when dealing with shape-shifters." Serena radiated excitement as she gave me the crossbow to look at for myself.

I stole a glance to see Anjani watching me. The sunlight made her shimmer, and her eyes were two emerald fires burning into me. I shifted my focus back to the crossbow.

"What's so special about this?" I asked, taking in all the sculpted details on the handmade weapon. The core structure was made of a lightweight black metal, on which cherry wood plaques with fine engravings had been mounted. My eyes followed the swirling patterns along the handle. This crossbow was meant to be shot with one hand, and the reloading mechanism was simple for the sake of speed.

"The arrows are laced with a special blend of poisons that are incredibly toxic to shape-shifters," Anjani explained. "The Druid's greenhouse has a few hidden treasures."

Draven smirked, his hand on Serena's shoulder. "We need to get moving, while it's still early," he said. "I reckon we have a day and a half before we reach the Red Tribe."

Serena took one of the duffel bags and hung it from her shoulder. Bijarki took the other one, and Anjani still held on to him.

"I'm coming with you," I announced.

All four of them stilled and looked at me, except for the Druid. But I was only interested in Anjani's reaction.

"There's no need. You'd just be in the way," she replied with a lifted eyebrow.

"That's nonsense. Draven's blind, relying on Serena. You're wounded as well. You need an extra pair of hands on deck for protection," I insisted. Tension bunched in my shoulders.

Bijarki narrowed his eyes.

I had completely disregarded him.

He cleared his throat as if to politely remind me that he was still there.

"My point stands," I told him. "You can't protect Anjani and fight shape-shifters."

"You'd be surprised at what I can do." Bijarki's smirk irritated me further.

"I don't really care. I am coming along. You need all the help you can get, while the mansion is safe under the shield. I'm of better use to you on the road than in there." I nodded toward the house.

A moment passed, while they reflected on my arguments. Anjani didn't seem pleased at all, pursing her lips and looking anywhere but at me. It amused me to notice how I'd gotten to her. Her mighty warrior demeanor was something I was keen to unravel. I wanted to see her soften up. What would that look like?

"We didn't pack enough food for an extra person," Anjani said, trying one last time to persuade me to quit. She didn't know me very well. She didn't know Serena very well either.

"Actually we've got a couple of extra loaves in the bag, just in case," my dearest, always-prepared cousin interjected with a smile.

"There you have it. We're good to go." I took a deep, well-deserved breath. "Are the girls watching over Phoenix?" I asked Serena.

"Yeah, hopefully he'll wake up by the time we get back," she replied. "Besides, Field's with them."

I nodded and stepped in front of Bijarki and Anjani, straightening my back.

"I'll take the succubus. You need your full strength and balance to carry that bag and shoot arrows at shape-shifters through the jungle." I smiled smugly.

Bijarki looked at me, then at Anjani, and back at me before he surrendered and left her wobbling on one leg. She looked so uncomfortable. I chuckled on the inside.

I swiftly stepped to her side, pulled her close to me, and snaked my arm around her waist.

She held her breath for a moment, exhaled loudly, and rolled her eyes. It wasn't necessarily irritation that I saw on her beautiful face, but rather some kind of anguish. I figured maybe she hated her condition, having to rely on one of us for support. The thought lined up with what she'd told us about her tribe and their customs last night.

Bijarki led the way toward the edge of the property, bag on one shoulder and crossbow in his other hand. A dozen short arrows with colored feathers poked out from the side of the bag. I followed closely with Anjani, while Draven and Serena walked behind us.

One by one, we passed the protective shield and headed into the jungle, where winds whispered and rustled the leaves and dangers lurked in the dark shadows. My chest tightened at the thought, and my hand instinctively pressed into Anjani's hip. I felt her body tense against mine.

This was going to be an interesting trip.

Vita
[GRACE AND LAWRENCE'S DAUGHTER]

Serena and the rest of the group had been gone for a few hours. Draven had left some instructions for Aida and me regarding our Oracle powers. Even with Phoenix out of it, two Oracles were still standing, and we should make use of the time while Draven and the others were away. He told us to tap into our visions further, using the herbs from last time, while Field watched over us.

However, it wasn't something either of us wanted to rush into. Both Aida and I were still reeling from the previous day's events. We decided to wait another day, clear our heads, and keep our eyes on Phoenix in the meantime.

I watched over Phoenix in the basement until Aida came down and told me to spend some time out in the sun.

"You're starting to look like a corpse," she joked and pulled me off my stool, taking my seat beside Phoenix.

I smiled. I didn't know what I would've done without her.

I went upstairs and grabbed a quick lunch from the dining room, then roamed through the mansion for a while out of sheer boredom. I found some candles in mason jars in one of the rooms upstairs and decided to go out in the back garden and try practicing some fae stuff. It sure beat wandering around a house filled with dead stuffed animals and old books.

I grabbed four jars with candles and a box of matches and scuttled downstairs. There was a big, beautiful magnolia tree in the back garden where I'd seen Phoenix before. It branched out with a thick crown of pale pink blossoms, casting a pleasant shade over the growing grass.

I sat down underneath the tree, my back against the southern side of the plantation house. The jungle unraveled in front of me in undulating shades of dark green and yellow accents.

The candles waited defiantly in their jars for me to fail miserably at controlling their flames. But Zerus's image formed in the back of my head, and I shook the negative thoughts away.

I looked around me and took a deep breath. I was surrounded by nature. My fingers brushed over the soft blades of grass.

I remembered the sentry's words the last time we'd spoken.

You need to slow down, to study the natural world before you can claim ownership over it, he'd said. I needed to take it easy as I often allowed my frustration to get the best of me.

I lit up one of the candles inside its jar and waited a few minutes. I watched the flame rise slowly, drawing in the oxygen that kept it burning. I breathed in and out, carefully composing myself as my palms hovered above the jar.

I willed the flame to react to my body, and it flickered just a little bit. Then my mind ran off, thinking about the Nevertide Oracle. I wondered how she was feeling, locked up in the glass sphere filled with water. I couldn't imagine anything worse than losing my freedom like that. To be blind and helpless while time flowed in and out of her with visions of everything past, present, and future…

I imagined the torture of living at the whims of a power-hungry Destroyer that had no problem shedding the blood of innocent creatures, as long as he got his way. The same fate would await me as well, along with Aida and Phoenix, if we didn't do something about Azazel.

The Druid had been incredibly helpful, despite his less than conventional methods. I had to give him credit. He'd dedicated his life to protecting Oracles, as had his father before him. He lived to keep us safe, while the world beyond the mansion turned darker and uglier each day.

Tears stung my eyes. The Nevertide Oracle was trapped in

her glass bubble, suspended in time, almost lifeless, yet unable to let go. I remembered the candle beneath my hands and looked down. The flame had gone out.

"Damn it," I muttered. I had to snap out of it. Instead of getting closer to nature, I was drifting away thinking about the Nevertide Oracle. No wonder I was failing every time I tried to bring my fae abilities to the surface; I was too easily distracted.

A few moments later, I lit the candle again and placed my hands above the jar.

This time, I kept my eyes open, my gaze fixed on a willow tree in the distance. Its branches brushed over the dark swamp water beneath it. I focused on the branches swaying in the breeze.

Slow down.

It didn't do much good. My mind wandered off again, this time—predictably—to Bijarki. Flashbacks of my recent dreams intertwined with memories of my visions of him—our bodies close, lips fused in ardent kisses while the world crumbled around us beneath the weight of giant snake tails and corruption.

Heat bloomed from my core outwards, sending currents down to my fingertips. I shook my head and noticed the flame had gone out again.

A heavy sigh rumbled out of my chest, carrying the weight of all my dreams and visions with it, leaving behind clear feelings of longing at the thought of Bijarki. Who was I trying to fool?

The future kept bringing us together. My own mind and body had turned against me, pulling me toward him with every chance they got. As closed off as I'd always been, there was no point in denying this any longer.

I was attracted to Bijarki, and—assuming he wasn't an outright liar, which he'd given me no reason to believe—it seemed to have nothing to do with his seduction tactics. It was all me.

My breath hitched every time our eyes met. I could lose myself in those pools of liquid mercury and deep blue. My skin prickled under his touch—in my visions, in my dreams, and in real life. His military demeanor made him come across as strong and incredibly attractive, on top of what he'd been gifted with by nature.

Why was I fighting so hard against him, against what I felt toward him?

There was no point. Muzzling my emotions was only going to make things worse, as already evidenced by my outburst that morning. Why not give into it? Why not just feel it all?

A different kind of warmth enveloped me. It felt like the air was pouring into me, filling my lungs as I exhaled tremendous amounts of pure relief. A smile lit my face. I looked around. It all seemed brighter, more vibrant and open to me. As if nature was smiling back at me.

I could feel it in the wind, the breeze whispering in my ears. I could smell it in the air, particles of wilderness and soft summer scents. I could feel it in my very soul.

I looked down at the candle. The flame burst back to life all by itself with playful flickers inside the jar. I gasped, overwhelmed with excitement.

I did it!

It hit me then, as I remembered Zerus's words. He'd told me to let go, encouraging me to live, to love, to open myself up and let everything in. This must have been what he'd meant.

I bent over the jar and placed one hand above it.

Unbelievably simple. Just give in to the feelings, and the fae power comes to life.

I moved my fingers around and watched as the flame followed the motion, more intense and fluid as it swayed and licked at the glass. I raised my hand, and the flame followed, a thin orange thread extending from the wax all the way out of the jar, an inch from my finger.

Happiness engulfed me as I let the flame dim back down and resume its timid burn below.

I'd finally found my answer. If I wanted to command my fae abilities at will, I had to give in to everything I was feeling, allow myself to ride the wave of my emotions whatever they may be, rather than ignore or shut them out.

To become the best version of myself, I had to first *be* myself.

How proud Zerus would be of me now, I thought with a watery smile. I just wished he and my parents could have been here, standing around me in this moment to see it.

Phoenix
[Hazel & Tejus's son]

I must be dreaming.

I couldn't feel anything. I could see and hear, but I had no control over my body. It felt like I was watching a movie in which I was the protagonist. The script had already been written, but I didn't know where it would take me.

The magnolia tree towered above me in blotches of pale and bubblegum pink framed by a clear blue sky. I saw the plantation house behind me, untouched by time or decay. There was a soft breeze blowing against my face, coming from the dark jungle beyond the swamps. Whispers and lost thoughts traveled along with it, brushing past my ears as if the wilderness was trying to tell me something.

I didn't know what I was doing there. Just moments earlier I'd been surrounded by bloodthirsty shape-shifters with nothing but the Daughters' knife to defend myself. The thought of Jovi and the woman he'd been trying to save from the swamp slammed into me.

Where are they?

It all felt like such a long time ago. I worried about him. I worried about myself. I saw my hand rise and reach the back of my head. I'd fallen during my fight with the shape-shifters. Everything had gone dark.

I looked around, but there was no sign of anyone. I wanted to go look for him. Maybe he was still in the swamp. Maybe he'd made it out. Either way my body didn't listen. I wanted to get angry and fight against it, but I couldn't even do that.

It was as if something had taken over my limbs and my brain, forcing me to watch whatever it was about to do with me.

I looked down. My boots stood on a bed of fallen magnolia petals. The familiarity of it all ignited me. The Daughter was beneath me, sleeping in her shell deep underground.

Is this a vision?

I had no other choice but to let go of my thoughts and see where it took me. My eyes were fixated on the ground. My boots started to sink in, swallowed by petals the size of my palms. The earth was slowly but surely eating me up.

I should have panicked and tried to claw my way back out, but I had no control over my body and a lingering feeling of knowing where I was being taken.

The world above disappeared as I was engulfed by darkness, dirt, and magnolia tree roots. The roots were a most peculiar shade of red, glowing and pumping life into the sleeping Daughter's shell. Under normal circumstances I would have suffocated, but here I was still alert.

Next thing I knew I was standing in front of the familiar shell. It had changed its appearance. Deep red veins crossed its pearlescent pink surface, drawn from the magnolia roots above. Whatever was flowing through them, it glowed in a precise rhythm, like a crimson heartbeat.

My chest tightened, the first physical feeling that I experienced in that state. My thoughts ran to her. She was inside, hidden from everyone and everything. I could feel her heartbeat resonate inside my ribcage.

Nothing else mattered. I just wanted to see her again.

I watched as my body was pulled toward the egg by an invisible force. The sensation of soft fingers touching my face lingered before I was drawn inside the shell. The hard casing didn't object to my body going through it. It dawned on me then that my presence was more spiritual than physical. Whatever I was feeling was directly connected to my very soul. The longing she'd nurtured in me stemmed from it.

A brilliant light glazed over me. I found myself lying inside the shell, facing her. The Daughter slept, curled up in a fetal position, her reddish pink hair flowing around her with no regard for gravity. Her body was covered in a delicate shimmer, its soft light pulsating to the rhythm of the shell's red veins, which converged into her back as if feeding her.

I watched her for a while and listened to the sound of her heartbeat echoing around us. It was calm and comforting. Her lips were a spicy red, glistening under the light. They parted slightly.

I could stay here forever.

Her pulse echoed inside of me, too, drumming in my ears, and I felt it accelerate as she opened her eyes. If I'd had breath at that moment, it would have stopped. Instead, I felt myself burn under her gaze, two pools of electric indigo storms beckoning me to surrender my entire being to her.

Her lips moved slowly, as if she was saying something, but I couldn't hear her.

I wanted to speak to her, I wanted to tell her something, but I had no control over my mouth. She kept talking, and I felt rage bubbling up inside of me as I became increasingly desperate to find out what her voice sounded like, to understand her.

But then something incredible happened. Her words started to resonate and emerge clearly inside of me, in my own voice, rising up and translating into electrical signals that my mind recognized as coherent sentences.

She was projecting her words into me, and it was a superb and intimate feeling, as if she'd reached deep inside and touched my very soul without moving a muscle.

"Wake me up, Phoenix," she told me, in my voice.

How do I do that? I thought as I watched her lips stretch slowly into a faint smile. Her beauty was out of this world. I would do anything for her.

"The knife, my darling." Her answer came tumbling like a rock, as I started to feel my body again. Slowly but surely I was drifting back into consciousness.

But I wasn't ready. I didn't want to leave her. I needed more time.

"I need you," she urged me as a sharp pain stabbed me in the back of my head.

Pitch blackness came over me and took her away.

Aida

[Victoria & Bastien's daughter]

The past twenty-four hours had been petrifying. Seeing Field's injuries and his subsequent drift in and out of consciousness had rattled me.

As I'd cleaned his wounds, I'd gone through different emotional stages, from fear to grief to anger and back, unable to focus on anything other than making sure Field would recover fully from those deep cuts. The thought of losing him had punched me in the stomach, and I'd been struggling to snap out of it ever since.

I'd slept out of necessity that night, as my eyes no longer listened and kept closing of their own accord.

By midnight, Field had already gotten up and gone out flying again, but I was still reeling from it all in the morning, which further added to my frustration. Not only was I head over heels for him, but I'd been faced with the prospect of losing him, and I didn't know how to cope with such a horrible feeling. Loss wasn't something that I was ready to experience.

I wasn't too happy about Jovi leaving with the group to reach out to the Red Tribe either. The jungle was full of dangerous creatures ready to tear into us with no hesitation, a fact dramatically proven the day before when they almost died rescuing Anjani. I took comfort in the fact that my brother was strong, fast, and a fierce fighter; his wolf genes increased his chances of survival in pretty much any circumstance.

The Druid had given us instructions before he left, asking Vita and me to keep pushing ourselves and to use the herbs to further tap into our visions while they were away. We'd said yes, and we'd meant it, too. However, as the sun rose lazily over the plantation house and as we looked at each other from either side of Phoenix's bed, both Vita and I silently agreed to leave the Oracle stuff for later.

She'd been through enough as well with that emergency treatment of Phoenix, and she'd been spending a lot of time watching over him. The kind of violence that we'd been subjected to over the past few days wasn't something that Vita was used to, and neither was I, for that matter. Training for

GASP and surviving bloodthirsty shape-shifters were two very different experiences.

I sent her outside to get some fresh air that morning, as she was starting to look worryingly pale. I'd watch over Phoenix for a while; it was a good opportunity to analyze everything that had happened and the way I'd responded to yesterday's events.

I needed to clear my head, and the cool, dark basement was as good a place as any.

I sat on a bed next to Phoenix's and absentmindedly watched him in his deep sleep. His chest rose with each breath in a slow and stable rhythm, nearly hypnotic. My mind drifted to Field.

I hadn't seen him since the previous night, before I'd fallen asleep. He'd given me a warm smile, telling me he'd be back before I woke up. Yet, he wasn't there at dawn. A pang in my stomach reminded me of my longing to see him, to make sure he was okay and that he hadn't flown into another bunch of shape-shifters overnight.

As if answering my inner pleas, Field emerged from the staircase, and I was unable to move at the sight of him. I watched him walk across the room with wide and heavy steps. His long, black hair was tousled from flight, and his turquoise eyes were fixed on me. I couldn't read his expression, but I could feel my cheeks burn as he closed the distance between us.

He stopped by Phoenix's side and looked at him. Concern was etched into his sharp features. His brow furrowed, and his lips forming a tight line.

"How is he doing?" Field asked, his tone low, as if not wanting to wake him up.

"Still sleeping." I shrugged. "It's a waiting game now and up to him to wake up."

He looked up at me, and my heart stopped. Every damn time he shut my system down just by looking at me. It was becoming a struggle to be around him, and yet I couldn't stop myself from relishing each moment.

"And how are you?" he asked.

I shrugged again, mentally slapping myself for being unable to say more. To be honest, I wasn't sure how I was doing anyway. Physically I was okay, keeping an eye out for any Oracle transition signs, occasionally glancing at myself in reflective surfaces in case more runes decided to play with my mind.

Everything else was a jumble of emotions tossed around inside of me, from missing our parents and The Shade, to worrying about Jovi and my friends in face of the deadly threat of Azazel, his Destroyers, and the jungle wilderness.

The most prominent of these emotions was, however, focused on the man standing in front of me, asking me if I was okay.

Field moved around the bed and came toward me. He stopped in front of me, and I prayed that he didn't hear my breath hitch at his close proximity.

"Thank you again for what you did yesterday," he said, his eyes half-closed. "You didn't have to."

"Was I supposed to let you die from your wounds?" I replied, my inner wolf feeling playful and snappy, anything to distract me from his devastating effect on me.

"Somehow I don't think you're capable of that." He grinned, two greenish blue gems drilling into my heart. He sat next to me on the bed, and the mattress moved under his weight. His arm brushed against mine, and I tried to hold on to my self-control. I had no comeback.

A few silent moments passed while we both watched over Phoenix.

"It's been a rough few days. I can only imagine what you must be going through," Field said, not looking at me.

"I guess it's a process," I replied. "Trying to cope as best as I can without flipping out, really. One day at a time, right?"

He nodded. "Nevertheless, you've been incredible, Aida."

I turned my head in surprise and found him looking at me. Heat washed over me, and I felt my heart pounding into my throat. He'd given me a few such candid surprises lately, and I was trying to figure out where they were all coming from.

"I think you're exaggerating a bit, Field," I said, my voice so weak I could barely hear myself.

He shook his head. "No, I'm telling it like it is. Your strength and resilience are admirable. You'd be an asset to GASP."

He'd never been so forthcoming about my GASP potential before, even when I'd spent hours tackling my brother to get GASP's leaders to consider me for official training and a slot in the organization. I'd spent nights reading through encyclopedias of the supernatural, trying to keep up with the guys on the theoretical side. I'd never given up on the possibility of joining GASP, even when I'd been told I was too young. Because I was half-human, Benjamin and Derek—and my parents, for that matter—wanted me to be a bit older before I made the official leap. That had never stopped me, though. I'd persisted.

Deep inside, I'd always wanted Field to acknowledge me as his equal. I'd yearned to stand beside him, to wear the GASP insignia with pride, and to show him just how strong I was, how far I'd come from the chunky little half-wolf girl.

With a single phrase uttered in the most unexpected moment, Field told me everything I'd imagined hearing for years, and I didn't know how to react to it.

"I guess I never knew I had it in me, huh?" I quipped lamely, while my inner wolf kicked me.

"Yeah, the best of us comes out in the most difficult situations," he replied. "Most of us don't realize how strong we are until we're faced with something that seems impossible to overcome."

I nodded, unable to take my eyes off him. Faint shadows flickered over his face as he watched Phoenix. He passed his tongue over his lower lip, then bit into it slowly. I instinctively mimicked his gesture, sinking my teeth into mine until it hurt a little—anything to keep myself under control.

"Maura and I broke up," Field said, knocking me out of my reverie. It took me a few seconds to process the fact that he'd just said that, and to me of all people. He looked at me again. "This time for good."

He waited for me to say something, while I tried to decide whether I should fake my surprise or just keep my cool. He tipped his head to one side when I failed to respond.

"You knew," he concluded.

A different kind of heat engulfed me, burning my ears. I was embarrassed and didn't know how to get myself out of this one. I had to explain myself to him, before he got any wrong ideas. I hadn't felt this awkward since I'd realized at the age of seven that all my wolf hair made me very different from the other girls in The Shade.

"Serena overheard you by accident when you were talking about it," I said slowly, eyes fixed on the dark green tiles on the floor.

He turned the upper half of his body to better face me, and I felt like I was in trouble like that little girl again. A mixture of surprise and amusement drew a faint smile on his face.

I braced myself for whatever he had to say in response.

"Why didn't you say something?" he asked.

It occurred to me that my guilt was misplaced, since the only reason why I knew in the first place was because Serena had told me. I took a deep breath and regained my composure.

"It wasn't my place to say anything, Field." I looked at him. "I figured you'd say something when you felt ready. There was no point in me being nosy about it. It's bad enough Serena overheard and told me about it. I had no right to make it worse. Besides, you needed time to cope, to come to terms with the situation. I can only imagine what you've been going through, but whatever it is you're feeling, it's yours and yours alone to either share or keep to yourself."

I surprised myself with my emotional wisdom, and, judging by the blank look on his face, I'd surprised him too. Several seconds passed before he reacted. Turquoise flames flared in his eyes as he smiled—a different kind of smile, one I'd never seen directed at me before.

My hands fumbled in my lap, and I puckered my lips nervously, pulling them to one side like a kid. My strength had slipped away from me so quickly that I once again felt all soft inside in front of a man who had been at the center of my affection for as long as I could remember.

"You've really changed," Field replied, his voice reaching new depths.

"Hm? What do you mean?"

"I think I'm looking at you, and I can finally see you for the first time. The real you," he said. "You're not the loud little wolf-girl anymore."

My knees were so weak I was grateful to be sitting down. I smiled and looked away, my eyes wet and my throat parched.

"Thank you," I whispered.

"Look at me, Aida."

My heart stopped again. I did as he asked, holding my breath.

His face was in perfect conjunction with his words; he looked at me differently, like he really was seeing me for the first time. His eyes shifted focus from my eyes to my lips, then further down and back up, blinking slowly.

"I never stopped to consider that even the loud little wolf-girl can grow up and become a strong, beautiful woman."

My stomach tied itself up in knots. I was unable to look away from him. Something blossomed inside my chest, expanding outward in hot and cold waves, and I chewed on my lower lip again, no longer able to use my brain. What else was there to say?

Field had always been the distant star I'd gravitated around for as long as I could remember. Maura's presence in his life hadn't pushed me away, but it had kept me at a safe distance, forcing me to cram my feelings down to the very bottom of my being. Upon hearing the news of their breakup, I'd desperately tried to ignore the glimmer of hope that was making all those muffled emotions scratch back to the surface. I'd kept it under control.

Then, all of a sudden, in that cold basement in Eritopia, in the midst of all the dangers and tragedies unfurling around us, Field sat on a bed next to me and finally acknowledged me as a woman.

Everything I'd kept locked deep inside of me broke free, crashing through the gates and drowning me.

JOVI
[VICTORIA & BASTIEN'S SON]

A couple of hours into our journey, we had yet to run into any shape-shifters, or any other creatures for that matter. The jungle was thick and dark all around us with gnarly trees reaching out above our heads and obscuring most of the clear, blue sky.

Various critters buzzed and crinkled in the foliage, while an occasional breeze swept over us and tempered the uncomfortable humidity. The road we followed was a battered old trail, previously used by incubi armies to travel between the northern and southern citadels. Shadows rushed through the jungle on both sides, but they kept their distance.

"They won't come into the light," Bijarki said, his voice low, as if reading my mind. He must have heard and seen them too. The incubus led the group, a few yards ahead of us, with one of the duffel bags on his shoulder and the crossbow loaded and ready to kill.

I was second in line, with Anjani leaning against me to keep some of the weight off her injured leg. The herbal treatment had fixed most of the damage, but her torn muscles needed a bit more time to fully recover. I didn't mind, as I was constantly in contact with her warm, voluptuous body. Her eyes twinkled in gold and emerald shards as they scanned our surroundings, crossbow resting on her right shoulder. She tried hard to walk on her own.

But every few steps I felt her giving her leg a rest and depending on me again for support. Her persistence for independence amused me, and I tried my best to be respectful and suppress my childish smirks.

My senses flared, not only in reaction to the potential dangers lurking in the jungle, but also to her physical presence. Her scent in particular, a mixture of freshly cut grass and mild spices, invaded my nostrils with each breath, making it a challenge for me to fully focus on the mission at hand. This succubus was dangerously beautiful, and I had to concentrate twice as hard in order to keep my head in the game.

Serena and Draven walked behind me, mostly in silence. She carried the second duffel bag, while the Druid used her other shoulder for support. Once in a while, I heard them exchange a few words, but I didn't pay attention to the details, as I was too busy staying alert while holding a gorgeous creature at my side.

Some time passed before I found something interesting to say. I'd thought about ways of starting a meaningful conversation with her, but every time I opened my mouth, I backed down, fearing mockery. Anjani brought out an insecurity in me that I'd never felt before. Whatever I said it had to be smart, and it had to demand her attention and respect. For a guy who normally didn't give a damn about much, this was new and murky territory, murkier than any shape-shifter-infested jungle of Eritopia.

"Tell me about your tribe," I eventually said, unable to bear the silence between us anymore.

I glanced sideways at her, enough to see a shadow of a smile animate her delicate, shimmering face. Her hair had been cleaned and combed to the side, pouring in charcoal-colored curls over her crossbow shoulder. It gave me a decent view of the soft line of her neck that made my throat feel dry.

"We're independent of the incubi nation in general," she answered, constantly looking around her, following the occasional moving shadows. "We live away from the males and from the so-called civilized societies and their cities. We've been doing that for centuries, long before Azazel rose to power and ruined everything."

I looked ahead at Bijarki, wondering whether he'd ever considered leaving the army and everything else behind to live in the jungle, away from the bloodshed and turmoil, like Anjani's tribe had done. His broad shoulders and firm jaw answered my question. The incubus had been raised for a military life. Devotion probably shaped his every decision.

"We live in the northern jungles, where few Destroyers venture," Anjani continued. "We hunt for our food, and the younger succubi gather nuts and berries from the nearby clearings during the day. We keep our distance from everyone. We rarely ever take a partner for life. We haven't had a male living with us for a long time. We send the sons away to live in the city and keep the daughters. We use the incubi for pleasure and to ensure our tribe's survival, nothing more, nothing less."

The last part stiffened my neck a little bit. I thought about Anjani and an incubus in an intimate embrace. I didn't know what was more awkward, the frosty meeting between a succubus and an incubus, or the fact that I'd spent an entire minute thinking about it.

"You only use men for physical pleasure and making babies, and then you kick them to the curb?" I replied with a raised eyebrow. She nodded, but I couldn't read anything beyond that. "And they say men are terrible." I smirked.

"Yes, well, don't worry, Jovi," Bijarki called out over his shoulder. "The succubi like us about as much as we like them.

They're wildlings who like to bite and scratch. Most of us try to stay away from them, but every once in a while, a poor sucker stumbles upon one of these tribes, and he's lost forever. There are cautionary tales about tribal succubi told around the campfires at night."

Anjani glowered at Bijarki. I wondered whether he could feel the fire on the back of his head. Her lips tightened to a thin line, and her nostrils flared. He'd managed to hit a soft spot, apparently.

I swallowed my chuckle as she narrowed her eyes at him. I didn't want her focus to shift to me in that moment; I'd felt the occasional wrath of a woman, including my sister, but never that of a succubus.

"With males like you, you can't blame us for not having much use for the incubi," Anjani shot back.

"We have no trouble finding ourselves a mate," Bijarki replied without bothering to turn his head. "Just because you ladies are feral and like it in the jungle doesn't mean there's something wrong with us incubi."

"So, how many of you are there in the tribe?" I quickly asked as soon as Anjani opened her mouth to continue the gender skirmish. I feared she'd eventually snap and shoot a poisonous arrow right into Bijarki's spine.

A moment passed as she regained her composure. It gave me enough pause to notice something I hadn't before. Unlike

Bijarki, Anjani didn't have horns on her temples.

"There are six families in the tribe, each with five to fifteen members," she replied. "Our strength is not in numbers but in our skills as warriors. We are trained from a very young age. We are taught that we must kill or be killed before we learn about how babies are made."

I found that to be more sad than chilling. I could picture her as a little girl with glimmery skin, golden-green eyes, and curly black hair being given a knife and told to kill. I looked down at her and noticed a fleeting frown before I changed the subject again:

"Why don't you have any horns?"

The look she gave me told me I had offended her, though I didn't understand how or why. Her eyes seared into me and narrowed slightly for an added dramatic effect. It sent chills down my neck.

"That's none of your business!" she hissed.

"It's because she's really young," Bijarki interjected. "The horns don't start growing on females until they hit their first few hundred years. She's just a loud-mouthed sapling."

I regretted asking the question, as I could feel Anjani's temperature rise against my body.

"Nevertheless, this sapling could still beat you into a pulp," she shot back.

"I would love to see you try, kid," the incubus said.

Her fingers clutched the crossbow tightly, and she looked like she was tempted to shoot him. The tension mounted, layer upon layer. Bijarki was obviously not afraid of her, but I didn't like seeing her angry. It made my stomach churn.

I looked around, trying to find something else to say. My hand instinctively gripped her side a little tighter, and my arm drew her closer. I heard her muffled gasp, after which she gradually relaxed against me.

"I'm surprised we haven't been attacked yet," I managed to say, clearing my throat and casually glancing around us.

"They can smell the poison from our arrows," Anjani replied.

"They?"

"The shape-shifters running around us. The other creatures lurking in the darkness. They can smell the black thorn-weed and deadly nightshade. They're not stupid. Most of them know to keep their distance."

"Where'd you learn all this stuff?" I was in awe of her. If only we'd known about these poison-dipped arrows before.

"It's part of our culture. We purchase or gather Eritopia's deadliest plants and infuse them into poisons of varied intensities, from tranquilizers to crippling pain and paralysis to instant death and everything else in between," Anjani said with peculiar pride. I figured this was her field of expertise. After Bijarki's comment about her age, she probably needed to reassert herself as someone not to be messed with.

"And this stuff kills shape-shifters?" I asked, pulling an arrow out of the quiver tied to her waist and carefully inspecting its iron tip, glazed in a dried dark purple liquid.

"Yes it does. Be careful not to touch it. It's extremely potent." Her eyes were fixed on the tip.

I couldn't help but grin. "Worried I'll die?" I aimed to make her smile.

"I don't really care. I just don't want to spend the rest of this trip leaning against that self-entitled incubus for support."

She was as fiery as an active volcano and seemed to enjoy verbal smackdowns. Once again, she left me speechless. I had my hands full with this one, and breaking through that hard outer shell of hers was not going to be easy.

I realized that I was eager for the challenge. I wanted to break through the hard casing. I wanted to get to her soft core and hear her whimper in my arms. The warrior succubus with silvery skin was hot as a summer's day, but I wanted to find out what she was like beneath that fiery surface.

SERENA
[HAZEL AND TEJUS'S DAUGHTER]

The trail leading up to the tribe was smooth, and we had sufficient sunlight to guide us along the way, despite the thick tree crowns stretching out above us. Even with Bijarki and Anjani commanding two deadly crossbows, I still felt on edge, fearing we'd soon be surrounded by more shape-shifters than we could handle.

I'd wondered why the shape-shifters hadn't attacked so far, but after Anjani told us about the poisoned arrows, my fear slowly subsided. Nevertheless, I kept my eyes on the dense jungle that spread out on both sides, on the massive trees and moving shadows.

Draven walked by my side, his hand on my shoulder. My skin tingled beneath the fabric where he touched me, but most of my attention was aimed at whatever was lurking in the jungle. Somehow, he sensed that and squeezed my shoulder lightly.

"It will be all right, Serena. Shape-shifters don't usually come out so brazenly during the day. What happened yesterday was a rare occurrence," he said in a reassuring tone.

"I still find it weird that they're not jumping us," I replied, looking over my shoulder.

"They can smell the nightshade," Anjani repeated as she walked ahead, leaning against Jovi with her crossbow ready to shoot. "Unfortunately my sisters and I lost ours when we went hunting yesterday. We were looking for it when we were attacked," her voice trailed off.

"What were you hunting?" Draven asked.

A moment passed, and a distant hiss sent shivers down my spine. Draven's hand pressed my shoulder again. His senses were incredibly sharp from those herbs.

"Shape-shifters," Anjani replied.

My jaw dropped. Looking at Draven, he was also taken aback, both eyebrows raised over his eye bandage.

"Their blood is warfare material," the succubus explained, noticing our stunned silence. I saw Bijarki looking over his shoulder. This seemed to be news to him as well.

"Care to elaborate?" Draven asked. "It's not something I've

heard of before."

"We discovered it by mistake, a few years back," Anjani explained, her voice somber and low. "A shape-shifter wandered into our camp one night and killed one of the girls. We reacted instantly and tore it apart. Its blood sprayed into the campfire, and it almost blew us away. It took us hours to put the fire out after it swallowed three of our tents. I don't know what it is about their blood that is so volatile, but we now hunt these bastards and drain them for it."

It took us a while to digest this little piece of precious information. Draven and I seemed to be thinking the same thing.

"This could be extremely useful in our fight against Azazel," he concluded, and I nodded my agreement.

"Why haven't you shared this with anyone else?" Bijarki asked.

"There isn't anyone else to share it with. Most of the incubi have pledged their allegiance to Azazel. We're not foolish enough to hand over such tricks to traitors," she retorted.

The sound of muffled footsteps approaching from the right startled me, and I stopped walking. Anjani, Jovi, and Bijarki stopped as well, turning their heads in that direction. Leaves rustled, and branches crackled as something came closer through the dark jungle.

"Speaking of which." Anjani aimed her crossbow at the

creature as it jumped out from the shrubs lining the road. The poisoned arrow shot out with a whistle and hit the shape-shifter right in the throat. It fell back with a squeal, then started wailing and squirming as the nightshade mixture entered its bloodstream.

I watched in awe as the creature suffered tremendous pain before it finally surrendered to death, its limbs twitching. It was half obscured by the greenery, so I could only see its legs and most of its chest and arms, translucent skin stretched out over raw muscles and sharp bones. More hissing came from where the shape-shifter had jumped at us. We watched in silence as the moving shadows stilled between the trees, then vanished deeper into the jungle.

"See? I told you, even if they do come, they don't stand a chance," Anjani quipped. "It's why we've been thriving up north for generations."

Draven's nostrils flared as he sniffed the air and nudged me forward. We resumed our walk and left the dead shape-shifter there on the side of the road. I left my tension behind as well. Anjani's poisoned arrows made me rethink our chances of surviving the trip. We were in good hands.

"I'm impressed," Draven remarked, and Anjani lifted the crossbow in the air as a sign of appreciation. Judging by the way she leaned into Jovi, she still had some pain in her shoulder and leg.

"And from what I can tell, that's not an easy feat to accomplish," I added quietly with a smile.

He turned his head toward me and sniffed again. I knew what he was doing and felt my heart tighten in my chest. His knowledge of my natural scent made me feel naked in front of him, despite his blindness and the presence of clothes on my body.

There was no better way to distract myself from what I was feeling than to resume my inquisitive mission.

"I've made it to Elissa's last entry in her journal," I said.

He kept quiet as we walked, his senses heightened and busy analyzing our surroundings. But I knew the impact of my question. I could see it in the tension drawn on his jaw.

"Can you tell me what happened afterward?" I kept my voice as soft and gentle as possible, in order to try and get him to open up more.

He slowed his pace enough to put a couple of yards more between us and the rest of the group and let out a heavy sigh.

"There was another page in that journal, but I tore it out," Draven said, prompting my surprise.

"What? Why did you do that?"

"I've read that journal countless times before you came along, and each time I smiled and cried and cursed remembering her and our time together. But nothing was as devastating as that last entry, so I tore it out. I couldn't stand the sight of it."

I waited for him to gather his thoughts and tell me more.

I placed my palm over his on my shoulder instinctively taking comfort in the feel of his skin against mine.

"Elissa wrote her last words to me before she went away. She had a vision of the present, seen through the eyes of an Oracle captured by Azazel. He'd used her to reach out to Elissa, and he was talking directly to her while looking at the Oracle trapped in a glass bubble. He told Elissa that he'd ambushed my father near the eastern citadel," Draven continued.

My breath hitched, as I was beginning to see where the story was going. My hand pressed gently over his.

"Azazel told her through the Oracle that unless she came to him of her own accord, he would kill my father and send back his head," his voice lost its vigor. "So, she left. She loved my father too much to let him die, especially after all that he had done for her. I was safe in the mansion under the protective shield, she'd said. At least I'd have my father back if she surrendered herself."

A soft southern breeze enveloped us from behind as we walked. The afternoon air was getting stuffy, settling in shades of purple and orange above us. I welcomed the breeze but didn't let go of Draven's hand.

"I never saw her again. My father returned a few days later, but he didn't know anything about what Elissa had described in her vision. That was when I learned how to make the fire that looks into other places," he said. "My father took me to the same room where I took you the other night and looked for Elissa. We weren't prepared for what we saw."

He took a deep breath, and his lips tightened.

"What did you see?" I asked. The whole world seemed to disappear around us as I waited to find out what had happened to Elissa. She'd been my beacon of hope ever since I'd first laid eyes on her journal. Her soft demeanor and genuine love toward Almus and Draven had even made me look at the Druid differently—less like an arrogant know-it-all and more like the child left on his own in complete isolation for too long.

"We watched her confront Azazel in his domain. She demanded to see my father when the Destroyers descended upon her. We watched helplessly as Azazel laughed in her face, saying she was by far the easiest and most gullible catch and that he had no idea where my father was. But Elissa wasn't a fool either. She'd taken a calculated risk. She knew there was a chance that my father wouldn't be there, but she couldn't just stand back and assume he wasn't there either. So as soon as Azazel admitted to his ploy to get her there, Elissa resigned herself to her fate."

"He captured her? That's what you meant when you said Azazel could manipulate visions, isn't it?"

"Elissa would have never allowed herself to be captured and used against Eritopia, against my father and me. She had a knife with her. She killed herself before the Destroyers could reach her. My father and I watched through the flame." Draven's voice faltered again. There was so much pain trickling from his words, it nearly broke my heart.

I could only imagine what the sight of Elissa's death must have been like for a little boy who'd loved her like a mother. No wonder he had a hard time talking about her. All the times he'd hesitated to talk about Elissa, all the times he'd pushed me away when I'd asked about her—it all made sense now.

"I am so sorry," I whispered, choking on unbidden tears.

A moment passed before he spoke again.

"You're the first person I've ever told about that day."

His confession stunned me. My mind raced as the meaning of his gesture sank in. He was opening up to me, slowly but surely, and while I expected to feel some kind of satisfaction in getting closer to completing my mission, all I could feel was grief and compassion toward the little boy who had lost someone so viciously and the man he'd grown into.

Furthermore, the realization of Elissa's death made it all the more clear why we needed to destroy Azazel—why we all had to pitch in and help save Eritopia. No one deserved Elissa's fate, the fate of those who stood against a maniacal power-grabbing tyrant.

"Are you all right?" Draven asked me, as if sensing my inner turmoil.

"Yeah, I'm just…so sorry," I managed to say. "Thank you for telling me, really. It means a lot."

He nodded, and we walked in silence for a while, until I felt the need to fill in some blanks from his account of Elissa's departure.

"Draven?" I asked. I paused, wanting to hear his voice and test the water before jumping in with more questions.

"More questions?" His reply caught me off-guard.

"Am I asking too much?"

"I think we're way past that stage," he sighed, wearing a feeble smile. "Go on."

I smiled guiltily back at him before continuing. "From what I understand, Azazel never captured your father in the first place. What did your father do after Elissa? Did he go after him?"

His hand slid off my shoulder, but I didn't let go. I held on to it as we kept our distance from the group. He didn't seem to mind, since he didn't let go either. Faint electrical currents traveled from his touch to my knees, softening them with each step I took.

"He didn't. I begged him not to. After Elissa left, I was so angry at her. I felt abandoned. For the few days that I was left on my own, I harnessed that fury and tucked everything I'd felt away in a dark corner deep in my mind. I didn't like those feelings. I'd been an otherwise happy boy, despite the isolation," Draven replied.

I was taken aback, gaping at him. This was the first time he'd talked about his feelings—not facts, not knowledge, not secrets, but his actual feelings.

What have I unleashed?

His fingers intertwined with mine.

"When I watched Elissa die, however, it all came tumbling back out. I couldn't control it. My father wanted to go after Azazel in a fit of rage. He'd loved Elissa. I could see it in his eyes. But I begged him not to. I couldn't bear to lose him too. My only advantage was that Azazel didn't know about me or the mansion, and my father had to make sure things stayed that way."

My heart sizzled, stripped apart piece by piece as the image of a broken-hearted little Draven with sandy hair and teary gray eyes lingered before my eyes. I looked up at him. He clenched his jaw, as if struggling to keep some details to himself. I had a feeling he realized that he'd shared more than originally planned.

I squeezed his hand, wondering if I could do anything to make things better. My eyes stung as tears of my own welled up. I wiped them away with the back of my spare hand and took a couple of deep breaths, distracting myself with the emerald green wilderness around us.

He squeezed back, and my pulse raced.

"Don't worry, Serena." He put on a gentle, reassuring smile. "It was a long, long time ago."

"Yeah, but you can't tell me it doesn't affect you still. I can feel it in your voice." I was unwilling to let him crawl back into his hard shell so quickly. He shook his head.

"It still affects me. Loss is never forgotten. But the weight of it dissipates with time. You'll feel it one day as well, and then you'll understand."

I wasn't ready to lose anyone yet. I pushed the thought away without hesitation. He smiled again, as if reading my mind.

"I can feel the resistance in your breath. You can't escape loss or death, Serena," he said. "The sooner you come to accept it, the more you'll learn to appreciate the little things, the moments you spend with someone."

"I'm not one to give up so easily," I replied, unwavering in my stride.

"No one is asking you to give up. Just enjoy every moment like it's your last. Do everything you would do if you knew that tomorrow was your last day in this world, in any world, for that matter. That's all."

His advice was sound and a blatant contradiction of everything he'd done and said so far. The Druid I knew was closed off and reserved, focused solely on protecting the Daughter of Eritopia and defeating Azazel. But the man holding my hand was filled with bottled up emotions and painful memories, secrets he'd never told anyone until I came along.

He gently tugged on my hand and pulled me closer, enough

for my shoulder to bump into his arm. His skin on mine felt so natural, and the way our palms fit together was as if we'd been designed for each other. I couldn't help but wonder whether there was more depth to what he'd just said about living every moment like it was my last.

Was his gesture a reflection of that? Was he stepping out of his comfort zone, reaching out to me? Or was I misreading everything? He confused the hell out of me, at first with his secrecy and now with his contrasts, but I didn't find it annoying. There was a thrill there, something I'd never experienced before.

I squeezed and leaned against him to see where it would lead.

"Nightfall is coming. We need to find shelter," Bijarki announced.

I felt Draven's entire body tense against my arm. I straightened myself while Draven took his hand from mine and placed it back on my shoulder.

The day was coming to an end, and so was our moment away from everyone and everything. Reality once again settled around us with a cool evening breeze and a myriad of crickets chirping.

"There's an old tree up ahead, where the road turns east," Anjani spoke. "Travelers use it for shelter sometimes, because it's out of sight."

The prospect of darkness and spending the night in the jungle didn't sit well with me. Shape-shifters were even more brazen then, and I didn't want to think about other creatures lurking under the moonlight. I didn't know enough about Eritopia's wildlife, but I was pretty sure most of it wanted to either kill me or eat me.

Sensing my tension, Draven squeezed my shoulder again.

JOVI
[VICTORIA & BASTIEN'S SON]

Nightfall came swiftly, covering everything in shades of dark green and black. The sky above, visible beyond the tree crowns, was a deep indigo with smoky cloud plumes stretching across a mass of bright stars. The moon was out somewhere, but we couldn't see it from our position.

We found the tree that Anjani had mentioned. It rose heavily above the others, several yards away from the curve of the road leading up north. It was flanked by an abundance of shrubs and tall greenery, along with several limestone rocks scattered all around. The ground beneath was riddled with mounds and steep holes hidden under the grass, making it a challenge to reach on foot.

The trunk was enormous, covered in moss and rugged slate-colored bark. Its roots looped in and out of the earth like the arms of a giant octopus. Its branches curled upward and outward, wavy and dressed in heavy purple foliage. It was a peculiar sight for Serena and me, but it was endemic to Eritopia.

"We call them purple giants," Bijarki explained as we left the battered road and headed toward the tree.

I had to be careful where I stepped, as Anjani had trouble jumping over all the stumps and rocks ahead.

"They grow for centuries," Bijarki continued. "This one must be at least five or six hundred years old."

"I've never seen purple leaves before," Serena mused from behind.

"If you think this is weird, then wait till we get further north tomorrow," Anjani replied. "The jungles around our tribe are quite… exotic."

We reached the *purple giant,* and I helped Anjani sit down on one of the curling roots. A large crack slit through the tree's base, from the ground to a few feet up, wide enough to allow one person to crawl through.

Bijarki lit a small torch, and we went inside to check it out.

Most of the wood had been carved out of the trunk for maybe five people to fit comfortably against each other. The raw wood glistened amber under the flame. It was beautiful, giving me the impression of standing inside a jewel. Other travelers had carved what appeared to be their names into the walls here and there, and there were a few leftover trinkets scattered on the mossy ground—a couple of metal pans, lumps of charcoal, and a spotted animal fur.

I figured the latter would be useful later that night with temperatures dropping every hour, so I picked it up and shook the dust off. It felt particularly soft, and it occurred to me that Anjani might like it.

I felt Bijarki watching me quietly and looked up to face him. He shook his head in disapproval, then walked out. He was still displeased with me taking a liking to the succubus, despite his warnings.

Well, it's not like I can help it.

I wanted to call him out on it but changed my mind as a thought dawned on me: I had found something and figured it would please the succubus to have it. If I was going to publicly insist that she had absolutely no effect on me, the fur in my hand stated otherwise.

Bijarki informed the rest of our group that the tree was good for shelter. "We can take turns sleeping," he said. "I'll make the fire. One of you needs to pull out some large weeds and branches so we can cover the entrance in case someone or something comes by."

"Something?" I asked. I handed the fur over to Anjani. She

looked at me with befuddlement, but I pushed it further into her arms, and she reluctantly took it. It felt like victory to see her accept something I'd offered.

"You should see what comes out of these jungles at night," Bijarki taunted me with a smirk.

A chill ran down my spine. I started pulling heavy fallen branches out of the nearby shrubs and leaving them by the trunk opening. I noticed Anjani watching me from the corner of my eye, but as soon as I turned my head to look at her, she quickly focused her attention on her feet. I couldn't help but smile as I resumed my task.

Serena helped Draven sit on another root and started collecting more wood for the fire, leaving the Druid to hold the burning torch.

"I feel like a piece of furniture," he muttered.

* * *

An hour later, the small campfire crackled in a hole dug into the ground and bordered with rocks. Bijarki sat in front of it with the crossbow armed and leaning against his shoulder. His eyes moved around, scanning the pitch black darkness that had settled around us.

Serena had taken the Druid inside the tree to change his bandage.

Milky white beams of moonlight pierced through the trees

above, revealing portions of the road nearby. I could hear crickets chirping and owls hooting and the occasional crackle of a broken twig as unknown animals tried to come closer.

"The fire will keep most of the predators at bay," the incubus said. "I'll take first watch on the ground, and you can go up in the tree and keep a lookout."

I nodded and moved to climb up the massive trunk. I'd made it halfway up, one solid branch at a time, when I heard movement below.

I looked down and saw Anjani pulling herself up on one of the lower branches. Her shoulder seemed to be in a better state, but she still had little use of her leg, as it hung limply in the air. Each move she made seemed strenuous and difficult judging by her grimace.

I stopped and climbed down a couple of branches, enough to reach out to her and offer her my hand for support. She looked at it, then at me, and slapped it away, continuing her burdensome climb like the independent warrior she insisted she was. I didn't like seeing her struggle, but I didn't think persistence was the way to go with her either.

Instead, I decided to go slow and continue my climb, waiting for her to call out for help when she couldn't take it anymore.

I made it all the way to the top branch and straddled it for balance. A few moments later, I was surprised when she pulled herself up and climbed onto the branch next to me. The moon was high and bright, and her skin glistened under it. She breathed heavily, and beads of sweat covered her forehead, but she still looked ethereal, her black hair framing her beautiful face.

I held my breath as I watched her settle on the branch.

She flinched when she bent her knee.

"Are you okay?" I asked, my voice laced with concern.

She nodded with a faint smile and took the crossbow out from behind her back. She pulled on the wire and set a poisonous arrow against it with a swift and firm hand. She'd obviously done this a million times.

We watched over the jungle around us. A wavy sea of dark green and black stretched out for miles in all directions. Lights flickered on the horizon at the base of a northern mountain chain. The peaks were dipped in white snow, which seemed brighter beneath the blanket of stars above. Thick gray smoke rose in a swirling column a few miles to the east.

"They're most likely travelers," Anjani said, looking in the same direction.

I had a hard time looking away from her. The sunlight gave her skin a silvery shimmer, but the moonlight was something else entirely. Anjani seemed to have been carved out of a large black diamond, with emerald-gold eyes, plum-colored lips, and long curls of ink black hair.

She shifted her gaze from the distant fire to me, and her

expression changed. Shadows flickered across her face as she looked away again. Her fingers fumbled with the crossbow trigger. She looked nervous.

"I'm sorry if I'm staring," I said, feeling responsible for the awkwardness that had settled between us. "I've just never seen a creature like you before. We have our own fascinating specimens back home, but none of them have silvery skin like yours."

A moment passed before she spoke again.

"Our kind is different even by Eritopian standards. If you feel in any way attracted to me, I must apologize. It's in my nature as a succubus. We are designed to seduce, and I can't do much about that. It's just always on. I can't stop it," she mumbled apologetically, taking me by surprise.

Where was the warrior I'd met earlier, and who was this insecure girl sitting in a tree next to me?

"Is that why you've been so snappy?" I asked, eager to get her out of that shrinking state.

I liked her more when she was fiery and armed with sharp comebacks, ready to smack me if I got out of line. In other circumstances I would have considered myself to be a masochist for poking at her, but with all the dangers lurking in the jungle around us, I needed her to be strong and brimming with self-confidence. Weakness never fared well in the wild; I'd learned that from a very young age.

"Snappy?" She asked, her voice low and husky and chilling

me to the bone.

There she is. I allowed myself to feel the satisfaction of a minor victory.

"There are other words for it, but I'm trying to be polite here," I replied carelessly. "If you're worried I'm devastated by your beauty and can't function properly, don't worry. I'm stronger than you think."

"So am I, so please stop treating me like I'm made of porcelain and need your help with every move I make."

I smiled mostly to myself, not willing to poke that bear again, and continued scanning the world beneath. We'd found one of the tallest purple giants in the area, giving us a great tactical advantage with its bird's eye view.

Some time passed before Anjani cut through the silence, her back leaning against the trunk.

"Tell me about your world," she said with eyes half-closed.

"My world? What, you need a good bedtime story? Getting sleepy?" I grinned, ready to irritate her into staying awake and alert. I understood that she was most likely exhausted from the trip and the climb, but we still had a few hours to go before Serena would take our place up here.

I needed my succubus sharp and ready to kill anything that dared to come after us.

My succubus?

"If you don't want to tell me anything, just say so," she shot back and sat up. Her lips were pursed, and she crossed her arms, crossbow still in one hand and dangerously pointed in my direction.

I moved back a few inches to get myself out of the way in case she accidentally—or purposely—shot an arrow my way.

"My world is incredibly boring compared to yours," I said slowly. "Yours, on the other hand, is a biologist's dream."

"What's a biologist?"

"The equivalent of your Druids, but less kill-y, more nerdy."

Judging by the confused look on her face, I hadn't done a good job of explaining the term. The cultural differences left a gap between us, but I was still very much determined to learn more about her and her world. I figured she'd open up more if I offered some information in exchange.

"A biologist is a person of science who studies and is an expert in all things concerning living organisms," I continued. "That means both plants and animals. Back in our world, they're still discovering new species here and there, but they've pretty much seen it all in multiple variations. If I were to bring a biologist here, however, he'd probably die of happiness. They love, absolutely love, discovering new life forms. All you Eritopians qualify as new life forms."

"I understand," Anjani replied slowly. "Here, the Druids used to be like your biologists. Until Azazel started killing those he couldn't corrupt."

Her voice trailed off, making me understand exactly how painful the subject was to her. I decided to dig a little deeper nonetheless. She seemed strong. She could take it.

"Tell me more about your tribe. What was it like before Azazel took power?" I asked.

"It was good. Life was good," she said, looking out in the distance. "I was born after he came along, but my elder sisters told me stories about what it was like before him. The incubi and succubi had thousands and thousands of miles of land. Our tribe wasn't the only one either. There were dozens of succubus tribes living out in the wilderness. We helped defeat many invading armies with our strength and prowess in battle and maintained our independence. Then Azazel took over, started killing his own kind and, when there were almost no Druids left standing against him, he turned his sights on us."

Tears welled in her eyes, and she wiped them away quickly, giving me a sideways glance to see if I was looking. I turned my head just in time, leaving her with the impression that I hadn't seen anything.

Something weighed heavily in the pit of my stomach as I pictured Anjani growing up in such a cruel world, where death and darkness lingered at every corner, where tyranny was the law of the land. I'd been so lucky in our Shade by comparison.

"One by one, our tribes fell, the blood of our sisters soaking the dirt. We stayed up north and limited our movements. We took all possible precautions to keep out of the Destroyers' way, while the rest of our kind perished or joined Azazel in order to survive. We borrowed magic from swamp witches and Druids, enough to keep our tribe out of sight."

"Swamp witches?" I wondered how they might differ from our witches.

"They're gone now, I think. There were a few of them living in the swamps surrounding the eastern citadels. No one knew where they were from or how old they were, but it seemed as though they had been around forever. Their great magic was passed down from generation to generation, powerful spells for protection and healing. We learned how to shield the tribe from Destroyers thanks to them. But after Azazel rose to power and started hacking and slashing left and right, they were gone, though no one knows whether they died or just vanished."

The more I listened, the more fascinated I became with Eritopia, despite its current state. Its natural weirdness and way of life were different from what I'd grown up with back home, even compared to what I'd seen coming from the supernatural world. The In-Between was full of mystique and dangers that could either save or kill me.

Neither is as enticing or as attractive as Anjani. I held on to that thought for later.

"How do you shield the tribe from Destroyers?" I asked, trying to keep my mind off the fine line of her neck. The curve sent heatwaves through my entire body.

"You'll see when you get there." She glanced at me, and her face dropped.

She straightened her back and averted her eyes, visibly embarrassed. It dawned on me that, despite my innocent questions, I was looking at her in a way that made her feel uncomfortable.

"Oh, don't tell me you've never seen a man look at you like that before." I chuckled, smiling playfully. I wondered if I could make her blush. Given her complexion, I was curious to see what that looked like.

"It's still leering," she shot back, irritation dripping from her husky voice.

"I thought you were a badass warrior succubus! Since when are you so sensitive to the way a guy looks at you? You ladies take pride in your superiority and independence, after all."

She threw me the deadliest look yet. Golden fires burned in her eyes, while a muscle pulsated in her jaw. She pointed the crossbow right at me. She was so intense, I started to think she might actually shoot it.

My breath hitched a little.

"Mind your tone. I may be injured, but I can still knock you out of this tree before you can blink and then watch you writhe in agonizing pain." Her voice was pure ice.

Once more, she'd left me speechless. All I could do was stifle my grin into a thin line and slowly raise my hands in a defensive and apologetic gesture.

It took her a while to point the crossbow elsewhere.

She could've followed through on her threat as far as I was concerned. Watching her beauty amplified from anger would've been worth every broken bone in the process—she was truly mesmerizing.

SERENA
[HAZEL AND TEJUS'S DAUGHTER]

As soon as Bijarki started the fire, I took Draven into the tree shelter to change his bandage. He kept quiet as nightfall settled, and I could tell from his slow movements that he was getting tired. I helped him sit down on the soft moss and stuck the torch into the ground for lighting.

He listened as I opened a duffel bag and rummaged through it for medical supplies. I took out a roll of clean linen dressing and a handful of thick pads made of a soft fabric I didn't recognize. Draven had given me instructions for packing the healing kit back at the mansion, but he hadn't told me much about which item was which.

I pulled out two small glass vials with clear, odd-smelling liquids inside. Everything in his medicinal pantry seemed to smell weird.

"Okay, I've got everything you asked me to bring here. What do I do?" I asked.

"You pour a little bit of both vials onto the pads," he replied. "They'll go on my eyes—or better said, eye holes—and you wrap the dressing around. It's quite simple."

I didn't like the sardonic tone of his voice. It didn't bring out the best in me.

"Good to see you're back to your old insufferable self," I mumbled as I sat on my knees in front of him and proceeded to unravel the old bandage from around his head.

"I never left." His smirk was a sobering reminder of how quickly he could sink back into his shell if I didn't pay attention. I'd only left him alone for maybe half an hour while I'd gathered fire wood. If I didn't know better, I would've recommended that he see a psychiatrist for mood swings.

"Yeah, I can see that," I shot back.

"Well, at least one of us can."

My irritation faded away instantly as I realized how terrible he must be feeling without his eyesight.

I'd completely disregarded his frustration. Even though his blindness was temporary, we didn't know how long it would be before the Daughters would undo what they had done to him.

But the more time passed, the harder it seemed for Draven to keep his calm, composed demeanor.

I removed the bandage completely, my fingers brushing over his soft skin and tousled hair. I held my breath for a moment, noticing the dark bruises around his sunken eyelids. My heart shuddered as I poured both liquids onto the soft pads and gently placed them over his eye sockets.

"Can you hold them up so I can wrap the dressing over?"

He nodded and brought his fingers up on top of the pads, over my own. His touch sent waves of heat through my arms. I withdrew my hands and reached for the linen bandage. His silence made it even harder for me to concentrate.

"So, what's the plan for tomorrow?" I asked, my voice weak but my mind determined to get me through the whole bandaging process without a hitch.

"Provided nothing kills us tonight, we will have another half day of walking north before we reach the tribe."

"Thank you, Captain Obvious," I retorted. I rolled my eyes and started pulling the dressing over his eyes, one layer at a time. "You can take your hands off. What I meant was what happens when we reach the Red Tribe? What's the plan?"

A smile passed over his face, so faint that I almost didn't notice it.

"The plan is to speak to the tribe chief and try to forge an alliance. Based on what Anjani has told us so far, they're one of the few factions still standing and in possession of some very dangerous weapons. Combine that with the three tricks up our sleeves, one of which is currently recovering from a blow to the head, and we will have a tremendous tactical advantage against Azazel."

"Will that be enough to destroy him?"

He shook his head, and I groaned, as I had yet to finish wrapping the dressing around his head. He stilled with a sheepish grin drawn on his face. Had he saved that grin from his childhood days, when Elissa had caught him with her journal?

The torchlight played with the shadow beneath his lower lip, further distracting me from an otherwise mundane task.

"Probably not, but it will show the rest of Eritopia that there are still considerable powers at play ready to stand up to him. It will draw out the others hiding in the shadows. After all, they can only keep hiding for so long before Azazel's Destroyers start coming after them. They're already tying up loose ends by hunting down rogue incubi like Kristos and Bijarki."

I nodded and tied the bandage tightly behind his head. I heard him inhale sharply and realized that I had drawn myself extremely close to him in order to see what I was doing with that knot. I felt his warm breath as he exhaled against my collarbone. A million shivers ran beneath my skin, and blood rushed to my head.

"You're being so good to me, Serena. I can't thank you

enough."

His words took me by surprise. I pulled back and stood up, putting the vials away.

"You've done so much for us as well, Draven. This is the least I can do," I said. I pulled two woolen blankets from the bag.

He leaned against the hard amber casing behind him. I gave him one of the blankets and sat down next to him, wrapping myself in the other. Draven covered his legs and crossed his arms, slowly relaxing into his position.

I felt the tree hard against my back. It was as good as it was going to get under the circumstances. My eyelids felt heavy, and a yawn got the best of me. The trip had sucked the energy out of me almost entirely.

I looked at Draven for a brief moment and felt tempted to mind-meld with him again. It seemed like the least invasive method to find out everything there was to know about him, considering his earlier accounts of Elissa's death.

I had felt so bad for asking, seeing how it pained him to recall those terrible events. At that point, sneaking into his mind with my sentry powers when he was sleeping would have done less damage than me asking more questions.

I was too tired, though, and it still felt like a horrible invasion of privacy. He'd done too much. He'd sacrificed too much for me to keep thinking about a mind-meld.

I shook the thought away and relaxed into the soft moss

beneath me.

"What are you thinking about?" Draven asked.

A heartbeat passed. *Should I tell him the truth or make something up?* I was wary of annoying him with my mind-melding thoughts.

"I was thinking about mind-melding with you again, once you dozed off, but I've decided against it. It's incredibly intimate, and you don't deserve me traipsing around in your head after what you've been through." He'd been so open with me about Elissa and the impact of her loss. I at least owed him honesty.

He took a deep breath and let it out slowly over the course of a few seconds. I turned my head to see the side of his face. The torchlight danced on his face, and I was hypnotized by the way it clashed with the sharp lines of his cheeks and the blade of his nose and jaw. The shadows drew my gaze to his lips, and I instinctively licked mine in response.

"It's not easy for me to open up," Draven's voice dropped to a soft murmur, warming me up on the inside. "Give me your patience, and I promise, Serena, I will show you everything."

My muscles relaxed, and my body slid along the wall until my shoulder leaned into his arm. I was so tired, yet the way he spoke made me want to try and stay awake for a little while longer. I hummed my approval as my eyelids finally gave in and closed.

I let my head rest on his shoulder, and I fell asleep to the sound of his voice telling me something else, something I didn't quite catch.

SERENA
[HAZEL AND TEJUS'S DAUGHTER]

I opened my eyes slowly, enveloped in sheer warmth.

I blinked several times until my eyes adjusted to the darkness around me. The torch had died out. A strip of moonlight poured inside the tree, making the moss floor phosphoresce.

This is no ordinary moss. I took a deep breath. My ribcage expanded as I inhaled, and I realized that my back was against something hard and broad but not as solid as the amber casing I'd fallen asleep on.

I was lying on my side, facing the crevice of the tree leading outside. Everything was still and quiet, except for the crinkle of crickets wafting in from the jungle. I moved until something tightened around my waist.

I froze, my eyes wide open, and my breath stuck in my throat. Draven slept behind me, spooning me. I was wrapped in my blanket and his strong arms with his fingers clasped on my abdomen. His body heat seeped into me from head to toe, and I lay there wondering whether I should move away from him or not.

Our bodies were so close that his heartbeat echoed into mine. He sighed in his sleep, and his breath heated the back of my neck, sending both fire and ice through my veins. I relaxed in his arms, and he nuzzled my neck.

His breathing was even, so I assumed he was sleeping. It felt so good, so right to be there, that I decided to enjoy the moment of absolute peace. His frame molded perfectly against mine. I felt a smile tug at the corners of my mouth as I surrendered to the feeling that was growing, ever so slowly, inside my chest—a mixture of pleasure and pain tying my heart in knots.

I didn't want the moment to end.

Leaves rustled outside, followed by a few thuds and whispers.

Bijarki rushed inside the tree. Jovi and Anjani tumbled in right after him.

My moment was over.

Their frantic movements made me aware that something horrifying was about to begin. Bijarki pulled a bunch of leafy branches over the entrance of our shelter.

"Destroyers," he whispered.

I jolted up and accidentally kicked Draven. He groaned, then stilled and sat up instantly. My hand reached out to the duffel bag next to me, frenetically searching for a couple of long knives I'd packed for the journey.

"How far?" Draven whispered to Bijarki.

My fingers grasped the cold metal at the bottom of the bag.

I pulled a knife out and clutched it with all my strength. My heart thundered, and blood raced through me like a rampant flood.

"A quarter of a mile," Bijarki said.

I heard him load his crossbow, and I looked over to Jovi and Anjani. The succubus held her crossbow ready, and something twinkled in Jovi's hand as well, presumably a blade, but I couldn't tell much with the darkness around us.

Bijarki had stomped the fire out. I could smell the charred wood and smoke.

"What do we do?" Jovi asked under his breath.

"We sit still, we don't move, and hopefully they won't notice we're here," Draven whispered.

I moved closer to the incubus, my knife ready in case the Destroyers found us. Draven snaked his arm around me and pulled me back. I tumbled onto him, unable to move.

My protests were futile. His grip was firm as he shushed me.

Horses galloped outside, their hooves thundering across the

soft grass.

I counted at least six. The Destroyers hissed as they rushed past the tree, their stallions neighing and piercing through the night's silence.

They sounded like an earthquake thrashing and rumbling through the jungle.

I stilled in Draven's arms. His lips rested against my head, soft and settled on my skin. My heart drummed in my ears, desperate to jump out of my chest and away from the madness. He held me tightly, unyielding in his grip.

A few moments passed before there was silence again.

Bijarki, Anjani, and Jovi breathed out sighs of relief. Draven relaxed as well, but he didn't let go, and I was too shaken up to move anyway.

The Destroyers were gone. We had been inches away from certain death.

Chills ran through me as my mind got tangled in the what-ifs. What if the Destroyers had found us inside that tree? I sank deeper into Draven's arms, instinctively seeking the comfort he'd given me earlier while we were sleeping.

Bijarki peered through the branches. "They're gone, headed east," he murmured.

"That was close." Anjani sighed and leaned into Jovi, who put his arm around her and pulled the succubus closer into his side.

I breathed in and out, carefully counting as I exhaled in an attempt to regain my composure. I could feel my hands and feet trembling from the adrenaline rush. I dropped the knife, my fingers sweaty from the grip.

While I may have been ready to face off against raging shape-shifters now that we had the poisonous arrows, I was in no way prepared to fight Destroyers.

Draven held me tight, his lips still against my forehead.

We stayed like that for a while. My fear sank back into the darkness, and I dozed off again, listening to the faint sound of his heart beating. Even after the prospect of Destroyers tearing us apart, Draven's presence managed to soothe me and guide me back to sleep.

JOVI
[Victoria & Bastien's son]

The rest of the night went smoothly. Even the crickets were silent after the Destroyers left. The entire jungle seemed to tremble from crippling fear as those monsters galloped through its woods, their horses neighing and their hooves thundering like they carried death in their saddles. Well, they pretty much did carry death in their saddles—death in the form of evil Druids with massive snake tails and poisonous spears.

Thanks to Anjani's alertness and Bijarki's rapid response, we'd been able to stomp out the fire and disappear inside the tree before the Destroyers reached us. She'd seen them from about a mile away, giving us enough time to climb down and hide ourselves.

After that, Anjani and I stayed inside the tree with Draven until dawn. Serena took her turn after a short nap and climbed up to keep watch, while Bijarki rested his head against the amber casing, closing his eyes once in a while for short catnaps.

I managed to fall asleep after a while, with my arm still wrapped around Anjani. In other circumstances she probably would have pushed me away, but instead she dozed off in my arms, and I wouldn't have had it any other way. Her soft purr and her hair brushing against my face were the perfect antidote to the adrenaline rush that the Destroyers had triggered in me earlier.

When I woke up in the early hours of the morning, she was already outside, changing her leg bandage by herself. I moved to help her but she shook her head sharply.

"I can do it myself, thank you," she muttered.

And she's back.

Bijarki and Serena had already packed the bags, and Draven was sniffing the cool air, telling us we'd have clear skies for the rest of our journey.

We resumed our trip, and several hours later we looked up and noticed the mountains towering over us—limestone giants with sharp ridges, thick pine forests, and snowy peaks disappearing into the clouds. The temperature and humidity had dropped a little, making it a perfect place to live—not too hot, and definitely not too cold. The jungle scattered where the mountain rose lazily toward the sky.

The sun was high above when we reached the end of the trail and walked out into a wide clearing covered in grass and wildflowers. It was as if we had stepped out of one world and into another.

The sound of running water lingered in the background, along with the trills of brightly colored birds and songs of what reminded me of cicadas.

We stood in front of enormous slabs of pale gray limestone that seemingly blocked our path forward. They were laid out as a wall that stretched from left to right for miles and miles in both directions. They were too tall and smooth to be climbed, and we didn't have any mountain-climbing equipment; Anjani hadn't informed us that we would need any. The mountain stood proud beyond, piercing through the thinly clouded sky.

Anjani left my side and went up to the wall. Her leg had regained some of its strength; her footing was more stable and relied less on my help. It was good to see her recover so quickly, but at the same time I would've been okay with her holding onto me for a little while longer.

"We're here," she said, then placed her palm on the hard surface. She muttered something under her breath, and the limestone started to ripple outward, as if it was made of liquid. "Follow me." Anjani looked over her shoulder at us, setting her gaze on me, then walked right into the stone.

It swallowed her whole.

Bijarki was the first to walk in after her, and I watched him disappear. I took a deep breath and joined them on the other side, followed by Serena and Draven.

As soon as I stepped through the liquid rock, it glazed my body in a cool, tingling sensation. The limestone particles gently ground against my skin as I took another step. The fresh mountain air hit my face, and I opened my eyes to find a different world unfurling before me.

The Red Tribe's quarters splayed along the base of the giant mountain, covering a few hundred square yards, perfectly hidden behind the magic wall. According to Anjani, few ventured this far north. She'd known which trails to take to get there, whereas most unsuspecting travelers would have gotten lost and perished in the dark jungles that covered the miles of uncharted territory.

"The waters are murky and treacherous and often covered in a thin film resembling grass, fooling people into walking across. They're swallowed and never come back out," Anjani had said on our way there. "And if the swamps don't kill them, there are plenty of shape-shifters still roaming around and poisonous snakes, carnivorous apes, and large *red-fangs* that will finish the job."

"What are *red-fangs*?" I had asked.

"Trust me, you don't want to know," had been her response.

With that in perspective, I couldn't help but feel grateful she'd been there to guide us through it all. But what waited for us beyond the limestone barrier seemed just as dangerous, based on what she'd told us about her tribe's customs and animosity toward strangers. We were strangers to *them*, after all.

A meadow spread out in front of us, flanked by the mountain's gigantic base. Large conical tents rose on top of grass the color of blood, which was littered with sharp black rocks and pink and white wildflowers. Animal skins were sewn onto these tents in various patterns of spots and stripes. Large curved swords and spears leaned against them by each entrance, as if ready to pick up in case of an attack.

They're always ready to kill. But who would be foolish enough to attack?

I took everything in, piece by piece. Dozens of succubi went about their chores in the Red Tribe, all of them tall and strong, their silvery skin covered in crimson war paint and tight leathers tied around their chests and hips. Their muscles were lean, glistening under the sunlight. The sky above was icy blue with white clouds scattered across it and swarms of small black birds undulating with the wind as they flew farther north.

Some were carrying chunks of dark violet wood to the large bonfire that stood tall at the center of the camp. The fire burned, and a thick column of gray smoke rose up to the sky.

Others were sharpening their swords with obsidian rocks and dipping arrows into bright green liquids that looked deadly poisonous.

Young succubi who looked like teenagers were busy skinning the animals from what must have been their morning hunt. The children were busy sparring with real knives in a couple of open spaces near the bonfire.

Serena and Draven joined me from behind.

Anjani stood in front of me, facing her tribe with Bijarki next to her.

We didn't move for a moment, Anjani allowing us a few moments to take it all in, but then one of the little girls running around noticed us. Her eyes widened at the sight of Bijarki, and she ran back to where she'd come from, shouting at every succubus she passed.

Soon enough, all eyes were on us, a variety of gold, emerald, and gray mounted on silver and crimson faces. One by one, the succubi stopped what they were doing and approached us in silence. Some took out their weapons.

Even with Anjani's presence, I couldn't stop my inner-wolf from firing up my defenses. I felt the muscles on my back flare up with tension as my fists closed, ready to strike if attacked. Even with Anjani's previous reassurances, the succubi looked as though they were ready to kill us if we so much as moved.

"I've returned." Anjani raised her voice, prompting whispers and murmurs from the back. "Where is Hansa?"

The succubi formed a semicircle, closing in on us. Their blades didn't go down, and I instinctively took a step forward, bringing myself closer to Anjani. Bijarki threw me a sideways glance and frowned.

"Don't move, Jovi," he whispered, as the succubi continued their advance.

"Where are your sisters?" A voice thundered from the crowd.

A tall, muscular succubus shoved her way through the horde. She was taller than me, I concluded, as she reached us and stopped in front of Anjani.

She was strong and looked like she had been sculpted, then carefully poured into a silver mold to preserve every muscle, every curve, and every sharp edge. A cascade of jet black hair ran over her broad shoulders and down her back in generous curls, and her eyes were storms of green and gold. Her smooth facial structure, her full indigo lips, and her arched eyebrows further strengthened my growing suspicion that she was related to Anjani.

Her breasts were ample, captive beneath a handcrafted gold chestplate, and she wore tight leather pants, sewn on the sides with thick red string. A scarlet-colored cape rested on her right shoulder, and a massive sword hung from her belt, partially concealed by the cape. One hand rested on the hilt. Gemstones were braided through the top half of her hair. They twinkled red and yellow under the sunlight.

"They're dead. Shifters got us," Anjani finally answered, her voice weak before the woman, whose face darkened at the news.

The tall succubus had to be the chief. Everything about her demanded respect and attention. Her stature imposed fear despite her enticing curves, and her glare made me want to shrink behind Anjani. I'd never thought I'd be fearful of a woman other than my mother, until I met this succubus.

I peered over my shoulder to find Serena staring, her mouth open, trying to take it all in. Draven, bless him, was still blind and couldn't see what had gotten us feeling so tiny and vulnerable. Serena leaned into him and whispered something in his ear, prompting him to nod solemnly.

I turned my head to see Anjani take a few steps toward the chief.

"The hunter became the hunted, then," said the chief, her voice rough and cold.

"I'm sorry, Hansa," Anjani mumbled and bowed before her. "We thought we could handle it. We lost the poisons in a fall, and we were out gathering herbs to make new ones when the shape-shifters ambushed us—"

"I don't need to hear details of your incompetence!" Hansa spat back.

I could almost feel Anjani freeze beneath her glare. I would've done anything to get her out of there, but from what I'd learned about her kind, it would've only made things worse. Instead, I kept my mouth shut and watched, ready to jump in if anyone tried to hurt her.

"I'm sorry," she mumbled, her voice trembling and almost tearing me apart inside. I clenched my jaw.

"What's done is done," Hansa replied, then looked to either side at the other succubi. "Tonight we mourn our fallen sisters."

They all nodded slowly, and Anjani stood up straight. Hansa then looked at us, and my breath got stuck in my throat. I didn't like her attention on us—on me in particular. She narrowed her eyes, and the eyes of countless other succubi zoned in on me, sizing me up with no shame.

I was starting to feel like a slice of fresh meat. I wasn't sure whether I should be flattered or scared. There was only one of me and so many of them. I'd barely gotten the hang of operating around Anjani. I definitely wasn't ready to deal with an entire tribe.

"Who are they?" Hansa asked, motioning toward me.

Why me? Don't look at me!

Anjani looked over her shoulder and gave me a reassuring smile, "They saved my life. Otherwise I would have died along with my sisters. They are my friends," she said and stepped back by my side.

Her arm locked with mine, and she leaned into me. I felt my strength return. My chest inflated with warmth and confidence.

I once again marveled at the effect Anjani had on me.

And to think just two days ago she was hissing at me, telling me to stay away or she'd slit my throat.

"This is Jovi. He and his friend jumped in and rescued me before the shape-shifters could kill me." Anjani continued through the chief's heavy silence, introducing the rest of our group. "This is Bijarki. He helped cure my wounds. And these are Serena and Draven, a Druid. His herbs saved my leg."

More murmurs came from the crowd, but a long moment passed before Hansa spoke again.

"I didn't think Druids were still alive." She cocked her head to one side and narrowed her eyes, as if unsure that she believed what she was seeing.

"I can assure you they're mostly dead or Destroyers now. I may be the last one standing," Draven replied as he stepped forward alongside Serena.

"How are you still alive, then?" Hansa didn't budge. Instead she crossed her arms.

"I've been under the protection of the Daughters."

"It's true," Anjani interjected when Hansa didn't respond. "They're protected by powerful magic. Azazel doesn't know how to find them."

"They?" came Hansa's response.

It felt like the more questions we answered, the more questions she had.

"There's a group of us." I spoke up, much to Bijarki's visible distress. He groaned and pinched the blade of his nose with two fingers. "The Druid keeps us safe."

Hansa's attention shifted to me, and my temperature rose. She was gorgeous, despite her intimidating height and muscle mass. I couldn't help but admire the way those leather pants glazed her thighs. Anjani cleared her throat. I looked at her and met her fiery glare.

I guess I'm staring.

I couldn't really help it. They were all so beautiful. Chances were they were also letting their succubus nature loose on me. I felt a peculiar heat rising into the back of my head. I gripped Anjani's forearm and squeezed tight in an attempt to anchor myself to reality.

She gave me an understanding look, and I realized then that the succubi were, indeed, having a deliberate effect on me.

"You saved her life?" Hansa asked, her gold-green eyes drilling into me.

I nodded, unable to utter a single word.

She walked toward me, and my heart stilled in my chest. I wasn't sure what to expect. Her hand landed on my shoulder with considerable weight, and her face, crossed by two thick diagonal stripes of red paint, blossomed into a wide smile. Her teeth were perfect. Her canines and the two slight horns on her temples were equally sharp and white.

"Anjani is my younger sister," Hansa said to me. "She will one day take my place as chief of the Red Tribe. Unless I am killed, it will not be for many centuries, but she is precious to me and to our clan. I thank you for rescuing her and for healing her wounds, young man. I—we—are all forever in your debt."

She looked over to Draven while she spoke, as if recognizing him as the leader of our group. I really didn't mind someone else getting the chief's attention.

"Name your price," she continued.

Draven took a deep breath and smiled, having heard what I knew he'd wanted to hear—the admission of a life debt from a succubus tribe.

The Druid didn't waste a second. "We need your help."

"What can I do?" Hansa didn't seem surprised, her hand still heavy on my shoulder, while mine persistently clutched Anjani's forearm.

"You know of Kristos, don't you?" Draven asked.

"Yes, the little rebel from Arid's clan. Couldn't fight to save his own life," Hansa said, her smirk denoting a seasoned warrior's contempt. I could see the resemblance in Anjani.

"He's dead. Show some respect," Bijarki shot back from the side, his tone sharp.

"Life is cruel," Hansa replied bluntly. "You're on my turf now, so *you* show some respect, incubus. We're not impressed by your kind here."

"We're the same species!" The incubus said with irritation.

"You and I are *nothing* alike!" Hansa didn't back down. Her voice thundered over us. "Not one of you incubi can face my tribe in battle. We crush men like you between our thighs for fun. Don't expect my sympathy when you're all crawling under Azazel's skirt!"

"Leave Bijarki out of this, please," Draven interjected with a soothing voice of reason. "He has lost everyone and everything to Azazel, yet he stands with us here, today."

A moment passed before Hansa and Bijarki curtly bowed their heads at each other to bury the hatchet. There was no room for pride in our situation.

"Kristos's father is about to make a big mistake and pledge his allegiance to Azazel. That is roughly five thousand more incubi joining his ranks, and we can't let that happen," Draven continued.

"He's weak. He probably thinks he's securing the survival of his men if he joins Azazel," Hansa replied, her voice laced with contempt. "I never liked him, even as a boy. He cried a lot and always ran after Neela's skirt."

Some confusion must have passed over our faces. Hansa's expression lit up with a grin as she looked at us. "Oh, you don't know!"

"Know what?" I asked.

Her hand finally left my shoulder, and I could breathe again.

Her touch alone could cripple my senses entirely, I realized. I welcomed Anjani's warmth seeping into my side.

"Arid was born here, into our tribe," Anjani explained briefly.

"Arid?"

"Kristos's father," Bijarki further clarified, and I nodded.

"As I have told you before, we only use the incubi for pleasure and to ensure the survival of our tribe," Anjani continued, prompting a chuckle from Bijarki. It was all he could do, given the death stare that Hansa gave him in response. "The girls that are born here, we keep and raise ourselves. The boys are sent to the surrounding citadels, to be taken into incubi clans that fail to have offspring of their own."

I looked over to the mass of succubi still surrounding us, each eyeing us curiously. They were all strong, fierce, and seductive—from the youngest to the eldest. Their way of life sort of made sense. It kept things simple and helped them maintain their independence. But I still felt sorry for the little incubi, who never got to see their mothers and sisters again.

"So brothers stay with brothers and fathers, incubi with incubi, basically. And the succubi stay with the succubi, separate from the males in all aspects of life?" I asked, still absorbing the concept.

"Yes. It's been this way for as long as we can remember. Arid was born here many centuries ago." Hansa took over from Anjani and pulled her away from me, wrapping an arm around her shoulder.

I suddenly felt cold and uncomfortable as more succubi turned their eyes to me. "We sent him away as soon as he learned to walk. Neela was his mother and my cousin."

"His other son, Sverik, is trying to persuade him to join Azazel's army to ensure their survival," Draven explained, and Hansa rolled her eyes.

"Sverik is a little wimp, even weaker than his father. And the worst part is that Arid may ultimately end up following Sverik's lead on this. To him, blood is thicker than water and heavier than his so-called warrior pride."

I could sense much contempt coming from Hansa where the incubi were concerned. I looked over to Bijarki and saw him keeping his head down, his gaze fixated on his boots and his lips pursed. He was clearly not comfortable, but I figured the succubi had their reasons to keep themselves away from the rest of the world and even their own species. With so many turning to serve Azazel, it didn't come as a surprise.

Judging by how pristine their settlement looked, probably preserved over millennia, the succubi cherished their way of life and stopped at nothing to protect it. I'd heard similar tales of independent warrior women back home, outside The Shade in the human world—like the Amazons of ancient Greece.

"Nevertheless, we need to reach out to Arid *and* Sverik and stop them before they do something foolish," Draven insisted.

"This has all come too far, and there is still time to put an end to it."

"So, what do you want us to do? Ride out to Arid and tell him to wait?" Hansa's eyebrow was lifted, a universal sign of doubt.

"This is about more than just talking to the few remaining incubi factions out there and hoping they won't turn dark. This is about forging alliances amongst ourselves, the ones still standing, and striking back at Azazel while he's busy attacking the last resistance cells of Eritopia," the Druid replied passionately.

"What do you propose?"

"Let's reach out to them first. I understand you have some extraordinary weapons in your arsenal. We also have tremendous tactical advantage right now. The odds will be in our favor if we come together. It's not ideal for any of us, but there's no time to be proud. Pride kills."

Hansa mulled over his words, while shifting her gaze from Anjani to us.

"Bring out the dragon tears!" she barked at the succubi in the crowd.

Dragon tears?

There was some motion and shuffling between them, until two young warriors came out carrying a heavy hemp sack. They carefully placed it at her bare feet. Hansa bent forward and pulled out a glass sphere the size of a billiard ball, filled with a bright red liquid, and fitted with a fuse.

"Don't drop it," Hansa said and threw it at me.

I caught it before it hit the ground. A sigh of relief fizzled out of me, and I couldn't help but glare at Hansa with raw anger.

What the hell is she thinking?

If this was the explosive that Anjani had told us about, why would she toss it around like a baseball?

"Are you trying to kill me?" I yelped, clutching the sphere in my hand.

"You don't strike me as a weakling who can't catch a little bomb." She grinned.

I handed the sphere over to Serena, who placed it in Draven's hand. I watched as he brought it up to his nose and sniffed it. He grimaced and coughed.

"What is *in* this thing?" he asked, clearing his throat.

"A mixture of poisonous weeds from the swamps and a concentrated infusion of shape-shifter blood," Hansa explained. "One of these is enough to incapacitate a Destroyer temporarily. Up to five are needed to create a blast powerful enough to kill it."

"How many do you have?" I asked.

"Enough to start a war, I'd say. But we lack the numbers to plant and ignite them where they can do substantial damage."

"And this is why we need to come together," Draven

declared. "Your bombs, enough incubi to lead an attack, and our Oracles can help us deliver devastating blows to Azazel, regardless of how many Destroyers he has. Once the incubi under his rule see what we can do, they will turn against him, and you know it."

Hansa's expression shifted from a jovial grin to consternation, her forehead smooth, and her mouth drawn in a small line as she looked at the Druid.

"Your Oracles?"

"I have three Oracles under my protection. Under the protection of the Daughters, to be precise," Draven replied.

"I thought Azazel had captured the last one."

"Not before she passed her powers onto my brother and cousins." Serena's voice was barely audible next to Draven. "Our mothers met her about eighteen years ago. The first born children after that encounter turned out to be Oracles. It's why we're all here, though we didn't exactly plan *this*." It was clear her last sentence was directed at Draven, and he lowered his head almost apologetically.

"Three Oracles, you say," Hansa muttered and looked at Anjani. A smile tugged at the corners of the older succubus's mouth. "I think we have enough between us to actually do something about that filthy snake."

Relief washed over me. We were one step closer to taking the fight to Azazel and rescuing my sister and best friends from a horrible fate.

"After all, it's only a matter of time before Azazel sends an entire army after us. Who knows how much longer we can hold out up here?" Hansa continued, her voice tinged with concern.

"So, you'll help us?" Draven asked.

"Indeed I will." She smiled and shouted over her shoulder, making Anjani cringe. "Kalli! Thenna! Riga!"

Three young succubi stepped forward. They looked a little too much like each other, and I was willing to bet they were triplets. They wore short, dark green cotton dresses and wide leather belts around their narrow waists with identical golden crests as buckles. They wore their hair long and silky, flowing in shades of black and purple. They were tall and slender, making me think they were very good runners.

"Pack your satchels, girls," Hansa barked at them. "You're riding out to Arid's camp. Get him to set up a meeting with us on neutral ground. You leave in an hour."

Kallie, Thenna, and Riga nodded simultaneously and rushed to the far eastern camp border to get the horses ready. Hansa turned her attention back to us with a lascivious smile.

"You all need to rest and relax now. Tonight, we *feast*."

She looked at me far too intently for me not to notice the sexual undertone. I then realized that they were all looking at me, Bijarki, and Draven, who, for all his blindness, was still considered a good mate. The succubi's expressions were excessively suggestive, and I felt my cheeks burn.

We had switched from political and strategic discussions to salacious double entendre so fast that none of us men knew how to react. The succubi scattered, but some sent me unspoken promises with their eyes. I would find out later what they meant if I didn't hold my ground. And so would Bijarki and Draven from what I could tell.

I looked over to Anjani, who glowered at me, then turned and joined her sister. They walked toward the bonfire.

To my right, Serena clutched Draven's arm, visibly flushed and looking at the succubi like they were bloodthirsty shifters. I couldn't help but wonder whether there was something going on between her and the Druid.

The thought left me quickly as Bijarki moved to my side and nudged me with his elbow.

"I think we'd best stay close to one another in case they get ideas," he mumbled.

I was in for a rough night.

SERENA
[HAZEL AND TEJUS'S DAUGHTER]

I was in for a rough night.

I knew it from the moment we set foot past the limestone barrier and the succubi saw us—well, had seen the men in our group, that is.

One by one they had stood up, coming closer and setting their lustful sights on Jovi, Bijarki, and Draven. I had felt so awkward, so out of place, and, frankly, intimidated. This was a tribe of creatures designed to seduce and weaponized to kill. I may be quite the fighter myself, but after looking at them, I felt small and meaningless by comparison. It was a feeling I suspected I would spend the rest of the night fighting off.

I tried to focus on our mission instead and couldn't help but smile at the thought that we were one step closer to putting an end to Azazel's bloody and destructive reign. It meant we were also one step closer to going home. However, that last thought didn't sit as well with me as it had in the past, because it instantly made my mind drift to Draven, wondering if I'd ever see him again after all this was over.

Evening settled around the camp, and I noticed a shimmering, transparent dome stretching above it. I hadn't been able to see it in the daylight, but it seemed to deflect light differently at night. According to Hansa, it was another perk of the swamp witches' protective spell. It was only a visual illusion that kept the tribe hidden from anyone or anything flying over. No one could see in, but we could all see out, like through a massive glass ceiling.

I sat by the giant bonfire next to Draven, leaning against a dozen soft pillows made from animal hides and stuffed with down from jungle birds. They felt good against my back, a welcome respite from the previous night's amber casing and moss floor.

Hansa, despite her imposing frame and thundering voice, was a very gracious host. Once she had seen the potential of our alliance, she relaxed a little and made sure we had everything we needed for the night. Three tents had been raised for us and stocked with water pitchers and blankets.

But before we could sleep, we had to sit through their nightly feast.

After a moment of silence to honor their fallen sisters, the succubi put the little ones to bed and gathered around the fire with massive platters of food—a dazzling array of weird-looking grilled meats, exotic vegetables and fruit, and what looked like local breads.

Some of the warriors took to the drums and provided the musical entertainment—an endless stream of tribal beats flowing into a passionate rhythm that further reinforced my view of the succubi as fiery creatures who rarely saw the fine line between love and hate.

Bijarki sat farther to my right surrounded by a throng of purring succubi. Two of them danced with each other in front of him, moving their hips and flexing their legs to the rhythm of the drums. Their muscles jolted with each move, and the light of the bonfire threw playful shadows against their silvery bodies.

They smiled at him, using fluid hand gestures to coax him into joining them, but Bijarki didn't react. Even with three other succubi lounging around him, their perfect bodies snaking along the pillows as they caressed his face and torso, the incubus looked into the distance, completely unresponsive.

He wore his eyebrows in a pensive frown. His skin glowed under the bonfire, his grayish eyes dark and solemn. His jaw was firm, and his lips were set in a straight line. He was truly a beautiful creature, carved to physical perfection. I couldn't help but think about Vita in that moment. I had given Bijarki a hard time at first, but really, she had every reason to feel attracted to him, with or without his influence. I wondered if his apathy toward the succubi's advances had something to do with her.

We ate well—though I found myself shying away from the meats—and Jovi and I were particularly happy, given the looks we exchanged during dinner. It was so good to be out of the mansion, tasting real food instead of the same magical tasteless junk we'd endured since arriving in Eritopia. I laughed as he sank his teeth into a large plum and almost growled as he tore at the pulp.

"What's so funny?" Draven asked, chewing on a hunk of bread.

I wiped my lips with the back of my hand and swallowed the food in my mouth. Before I could respond, the succubi brought over gold pitchers and goblets for us to drink from. I clasped my hand around the chalice, sniffing the pale pink liquid inside. It smelled like roses and spice.

"It's just that Jovi and I are really happy to eat food from outside of the mansion right now." I laughed lightly, then cleared my throat and resumed a serious and respectful tone. "Not that we don't like eating at the mansion. We do appreciate your kindness and generosity but—"

"But it tastes like crap, as you would so gently put it," he interrupted me with a familiar smirk. I blushed, a wave of relief washing over me, thankful that he couldn't see my face in that moment.

"Well, you know, when you have the same thing every single day, it gets drab fast," I said and took a sip of my drink.

His nostrils flared. "What are you drinking?"

"I don't know, the succubi are serving it," I replied after another gulp. It was sweet, but it rolled down my throat with a refreshing aftertaste. "Want some?"

He nodded, and I handed him a goblet.

The drum music tangled with the sound of firewood crackling and the cheers of the succubi. Now more of them were dancing and making use of their hips to draw the attention of Bijarki and, from the looks of it, Jovi too.

Jovi had been left on his own to eat and drink in peace. But that didn't last long, as he was swiftly flanked by two young succubi who poured him another drink and fed him morsels of food. He didn't seem to mind. He laughed, ate, and drank his way through the succubi party like a young prince.

I kept myself close to Draven and dined in silence, while Hansa and Anjani were busy catching up on the other side of the bonfire. They threw the occasional glance our way and curtly nodded when our eyes met.

A few hours in, I felt a little light-headed. My senses expanded, and I could hear, see, smell, and taste everything a million times better. I smelled the sweat trickling down the bare spine of a dancing succubus, the plethora of roses and sweet spices in my drink, and the soft hint of musk and leather coming from Draven.

I heard the heartbeats of all the succubi around me, drumming against my ears. I turned my head to look at Draven, and his pulse echoed in my head and resonated in my chest.

I looked into the distance and saw small animals rushing through the tall purple grass beyond the camp in pitch black darkness. Without using my True Sight.

What is happening here?

"I think there's something wrong with me," I said mostly to myself.

"What do you mean?" Draven asked, his voice low with concern.

"My senses are amped up like crazy. I can see, like really *see,* without my sentry powers. I can smell the most peculiar things. I can…I can hear your heartbeat." I breathed the last part out, and his lips curved into a smile.

"It must be the drink," his hand sought mine and his fingers brushed over my skin, once again sending trillions of shivers down my spine. His touch was amplified as well, triggering new and profound reactions from the depths of my body, electrical currents coming in wave after wave. My breath halted.

"What kind of drink is this?" I lifted the goblet in my hand

and placed it on the table. I'd stick to water from now on.

"The succubi are known not only for their seductive nature, but also for their celebration of pure life and freedom. Their potions have been perfected over time to amplify one's senses. It's what makes them such good hunters and fighters," Draven explained. "I'm guessing this is one of their concoctions."

"Wow, so this is pretty much what you experience from your smelly herbs, right?"

He laughed, and I melted at the sound of it.

"In a nutshell yes, but my state is slightly deeper, more detailed," he replied.

"You smell like musk and… something heady, like leather," I said. I'd just felt the need to say it, remembering how he'd described my own fragrance the other night. I could finally reciprocate the intimate gesture.

He stilled, his hand covering mine. I wasn't sure he was breathing at that moment, but I could feel his attention on me. He didn't need eyes to make me feel like I was under a microscope. My heart started racing as I tried to keep my emotions under control. His head tilted to one side.

"Your heart is galloping, Serena. What is it?"

I took a deep breath, trying to will myself back under control.

As much as I disliked it, I was saved by a succubus, who came and sat with us. She wore a soft, translucent white dress that covered her trunk but kept her long legs and arms bare. She was adorned with heavy silver and gemstones.

Draven straightened his back and let go of my hand.

I had a hard time taking my eyes off of her as she leered at him.

Her hair was long and straight, its color a metallic shade of red. Her eyes were almond-shaped and twinkled like sapphires. Her lips were full and glossy red. She was dressed to seduce, and she seemed to fully embrace her nature, wearing a dazzling, self-assured smile.

My throat closed when I realized that I was completely invisible to her. She ran her fingers down Draven's arm.

"You look too good to be true," the succubus purred in his ear, making me flush and curse the effects of that spicy rose drink. My hearing was too good now.

"Thank you," Draven replied politely, his tone a little too low for my taste. I had a feeling he wasn't immune to her charms.

Slowly but surely, my blood began to simmer.

"Would you like to share him with me?" She suddenly looked at me and put on that brilliant and seductive smile that almost made me say yes, until my heart twisted inside my chest, and I snapped.

"Hell no!" I growled at her.

I felt Draven's knee subtly knock mine, but I was far too mad to pay him any attention. The succubus looked at me with shock, as if she hadn't expected me to turn her down.

Talk about entitlement!

"I'm sorry, but we just want to finish eating and sleep tonight," Draven interjected in a neutral tone. "Thank you, nonetheless."

I was relieved.

The succubus looked at him, then at me again before she let a deep sigh roll out of her voluptuous chest and put on a polite smile.

"Oh well," she said and used her thumb to smudge a little bit of the red gloss from her lips on his forehead, right at the center above his eyebrows. "I understand and respect your decision. Contrary to popular belief, we succubi know to back down when a man is in love and loyal to his mate."

My face caught fire, my ears burned, and I had to take a few deep breaths to keep a straight face as the succubus dropped a kiss on Draven's temple, threw me a wink, stood, and swayed to the other side of the bonfire.

I looked back at Draven, and I couldn't help but smile a little. He'd been taken by surprise as well. His lips were pressed together, his hands fumbled in his lap, and his frame was awkwardly stiff, like he'd been frozen in a defensive position. Judging by how his own heart was racing—thank you spicy rose potion—he was either aroused or flabbergasted.

I prayed for the latter. I didn't like the feeling I got from the succubus's close proximity to Draven. I didn't like the way she'd looked at him or the way she'd touched him. I didn't like the way I'd reacted to her proposal either—so rash, so sharp!

Most importantly, I didn't like the way the other succubi were looking at him and me as if waiting for me to leave his side so they could pounce.

In your dreams.

We ate the rest of our meal in silence. Neither of us seemed willing to talk about what the succubus had said, not even to correct her assumption regarding love and mates. I would have addressed the issue if I'd had any courage left. But I had been sucked dry as the spicy rose potion really sank in and relaxed my every muscle.

I stuffed another slice of fruit in my mouth and chewed, taking deep breaths in between and trying to tune out everything I was hearing except for his heartbeat.

That I wanted to hear more of.

Jovi
[Victoria & Bastien's son]

Somehow I'd gotten separated from Bijarki and Serena during dinner preparations. I wasn't too far from them where I had been seated, but I was still pretty much on my own. As the drums started playing, and the succubi brought out the food, however, I got busy eating and nearly forgot about my vulnerability as a male in the midst of all those warrior females.

I feasted like a king, welcoming the taste of unknown but delicious food. The mansion food had been good for sustenance, but the taste had sucked the joy out of eating. Thanks to the succubi I had rediscovered the pleasure of sinking my teeth into something that didn't taste like boiled, bland weeds.

I'd noticed the same joy on Serena's face as we both stuffed our faces with what the succubi offered fresh off the fire pit. My favorites were the plums—or whatever they were. They resembled plums, anyway, so soft and juicy that it felt like biting into little chunks of heaven.

They brought out a special drink as well in gold pitchers. It tasted like liquid roses with spice accents that cooled me on the inside as I drank cup after cup. After another brief moment of silence to honor those killed in the jungle, the succubi started dancing. I found it interesting how they didn't wail and cry over their fallen sisters.

"We don't shed tears for those of us who die. We celebrate their lives, and we celebrate life for ourselves instead," Anjani had told me earlier.

The rose drink made me feel funny. My fingers and toes tingled, and my senses were amplified. As a half-wolf, I already had a spectacular sense of sight and smell, but whatever was in that drink cranked everything up even more. I could see little animals rummaging through the dark red grass, catching crickets and swallowing them whole. They had to have been about a mile away toward the western edge of the meadow where another mountain rose.

I could hear the exchange between Anjani and Hansa on the other side of the bonfire as if they were standing right next to me.

"If you trust them, sister, I trust them as well," Hansa was telling Anjani. I could hear her chewing on the roasted leg of some creature they'd hunted earlier in the day. I could smell the meat from where I sat.

"I do, Hansa. I was ready to kill myself if they tried anything against me when they first brought me to their house," Anjani replied.

My stomach churned. I didn't know she would've resorted to such final measures, had she considered us a threat, or me, particularly, after I'd saved her life.

"They didn't trust me either, and they were so fearful that they tied me down. But they treated my wounds. They fed me, gave me water, kept watch, and brought me back here in one piece. They're good people, Hansa. And they are right. We are stronger together."

"The Oracles are something extraordinary to have against Azazel. We need to keep these people close. I know we don't normally associate with outsiders but—"

"Desperate times, right?"

"Pretty much." Hansa laughed. "I'm sorry our sisters won't be able to see better days…"

Hansa's voice trailed off as she threw the bone into the fire and started working her way through another from her plate. I heard Anjani's breath falter at the mention of her sisters.

"I am sorry, Hansa. I tried so hard to keep them safe. Nayla was reckless and lost the poisons while jumping over the swamp. She lost her footing and fell in, and Shari and I fought hard to get her out of there alive. I guess the shape-shifters realized that we had run out of poison once they couldn't smell it anymore and came at us. We didn't stand a chance with so many of them." Anjani's voice trembled.

Hansa nodded and gnawed on the second bone. "I do not hold you solely responsible. The dead share the blame as well. Learn from these mistakes and be a better succubus, a stronger sister to your tribe. One day this will all be yours, and I'll be damned if I'll hand anything over to a doe-eyed weakling." Hansa smirked and nudged Anjani with her elbow.

I smiled, mostly to myself, thinking that this exchange was probably as close as succubi sisters were ever going to get, given their way of life.

I'd been so busy listening to them that I didn't notice the two voluptuous and absolutely gorgeous succubi who sat next to me on each side. They purred and smiled at me—perfect creatures with shimmering skin, long hair the color of an orange sunset, and luscious purple lips. Their eyes were hooded, but I could still see specks of silver and red swirling. They smelled incredible, a mesmerizing mixture of flowers and citrus leaves.

I took deep breaths, allowing their scent to fill my lungs and further expand my senses. I had very little control over what I was doing. Whether it had been my choice or the succubi's effect, I wasn't sure, but I was enjoying every moment, my mind numb and my mouth stretched into what I guessed was a goofy smile. I caught a glimpse of myself reflected on one of the golden pitchers. Yes. Goofy.

"You're so handsome," one of the succubi hummed in my ear.

My breath hitched as she bit the lobe with playful licks of her tongue. My skin fizzled, and a familiar heat spread through my body from the pit of my stomach.

"Thank you, thank you very much," I heard myself say.

"We should enjoy the rest of the night together," the other succubus whispered, her face less than an inch from mine.

"There are so many things we could do until sunrise," the first one said.

"We've never met a creature like you, Jovi. Consider us fascinated and very, very attracted."

I didn't know what to say.

Well, I did know. The answer was supposed to be *no*. But my body wasn't listening. My mouth gaped, but the word stuck somewhere in the back of my throat. My arousal was almost painful, sending shivers up my spine.

Someone pulled me up with surprising force—or maybe I was so weak that I allowed myself to get hauled to my feet. I looked to my right and saw Anjani. She was fuming. Her eyes had narrowed to slits. Her soft lips were drawn into a thin line, and her nostrils flared. I'd never seen her so furious.

"Keep your hands off him, sisters. I've claimed this one as mine, and I'm not sharing!" she barked at the succubi.

My heart jumped.

The gorgeous creatures frowned, then shrugged and stood up, pouting with disappointment. Anjani grabbed my arm and dragged me into one of the tents that had been raised for us. I was dazzled and didn't register much along the way.

She had proclaimed some sort of ownership over me. Even in my hazy state, I'd heard her loud and clear. As she pulled a heavy fur cover over the tent's entrance, I found myself standing right behind her, smiling. My blood raced through my veins, and my eyes couldn't leave the wonderful sight of her.

Whatever had been in that drink, on top of whatever the succubi had been doing to me, it put me in a strangely euphoric state, in which I had little control over my actions and felt like the happiest and most valiant creature in Eritopia. Nothing could stop me.

She tied the fur cover tight to keep everybody out.

I heard myself chuckle like a boy as I ran my fingers through her hair, a cascade of jet black curls pouring down her back. My gesture startled her, and she turned to face me. She looked stunned, her golden-green eyes wide. Her skin almost glowed, as if infused with millions of diamonds. I'd never seen that before either. Her rapid pulse and thundering heartbeat banged in my eardrums.

"What do you think you're doing?" Anjani hissed.

"Why are you glowing like that?" I asked and reached out to touch her cheek.

She is so beautiful.

She pushed me hard, knocking the air out of my lungs. I fell backward and hit the soft blankets and pillows behind me with a muffled thud. I held my breath as she walked toward me.

I looked up at her, towering and glowing, as if she'd been sculpted out of star stuff. Despite my hazy state, one thing was certain: I would have worshipped a goddess like her. I would have celebrated every inch of that perfect skin, every twinkle, and every breath that she took. I wanted her. Badly.

But my body was getting numb.

"You're under the influence of *sigala* and pretty much the whole succubi tribe right now. You don't know what you're doing," Anjani said to me, her voice like liquid ice.

"*Sigala?*" I heard myself ask, my voice low and echoing in my head.

"The drink you've been guzzling like water, you reckless boy! You've had too much of it! It's supposed to enhance your senses, but if you drink an entire pitcher like you did, it has a very different effect. Especially if there are dozens of succubi projecting their attraction on you!"

"You sound mad."

"Of course I'm mad! I didn't claim you for myself! I claimed you so I could rescue you from my sisters without looking like a fool and without fighting them off!"

I took a deep breath, the realization starting to sink in. The drink's effect was becoming obvious, as was my subsiding arousal from my brief encounter with the two succubi outside.

"You don't want me," I mumbled with disappointment.

She let out a long, tortured sigh.

"It's not that, Jovi. I can't control myself around you. I have a hard time keeping my nature from playing with your senses, so I can't be sure of what you're saying or feeling toward me. You have no idea how difficult it is to not know whether someone likes you for you or because your succubus features make them like you."

She crossed to the other side of the tent and sat down, bringing her knees to her chest. I watched her quietly as her diamond glow gradually dimmed.

"I don't know what it's like for you," she said slowly. "But for me it hasn't been easy. I'm taught that feelings are for weaklings, that my succubus nature is designed for pleasure and procreation, not for emotions. And yes, Bijarki is right. I am young. I'm too young to understand a lot of things, too young to be as tough as Hansa and treat males like I'm supposed to."

My mind was moving in slow motion, but even so I noticed a gap between what had just happened outside and what she was telling me. And since my tongue was so loose under the perfect excuse of *sigala* and succubi effects, I decided to bridge the gap.

"What does that have to do with you claiming me in front of your sisters?" I asked.

"I didn't claim you because *I want you*. If you're ever to come to me, it will be because *you* want to. Not because *I* want to. And certainly not because it's my succubus nature that draws you to me. It can't be, because I try so hard to keep it from influencing you. And it's so hard."

Her voice trailed off as she lowered her head, hiding her face behind her knees.

I was speechless, still trying to untangle what she was telling me. My brain was so damn slow.

"I'm not sure right now. I'm not sure if you touched my hair because you wanted to or because my nature is drawing you in. And I will never, ever claim you because I want you. Get that through your thick head," she continued.

I had no control over what came out of my mouth in that moment. Something deep inside of me had taken over. "I do like you."

Judging by how my stomach churned, my wolf instinct kicked in immediately afterward, slapping the human side of me silly as soon as I had said those words.

Her head shot up, eyes wide open.

"Whether it's because of your succubus-whatever or because

of you, I'm pretty sure it's the same thing," I mumbled. My eyes closed. My body felt like it weighed a ton. I struggled to open my eyes.

A faint smile quickly passed over her face. It was the last thing I saw before my eyelids gave in.

"Being a succubus is an integral part of you, Anjani. You should embrace that. I don't care why I'm so attracted to you, but I can't deny it. It's a part of *me*..."

Darkness enveloped me, along with a very sweet and familiar sensation, something I'd felt coming from her before when we'd been up in the tree and when we'd fallen asleep beneath it.

My head spun while I drifted off into my dreams.

I didn't get to hear her reply.

Serena
[Hazel and Tejus's daughter]

Not long after Draven had rejected the succubi and wound up with a red smudge from her lips on his forehead, others tried to join us. They laughed and danced and poured more of the spicy rose drink in our goblets. At least six other succubi tried seducing Draven in front of me over the course of an hour.

Some had been "gracious" enough to invite me to join them, while others had courteously suggested to Draven that they go somewhere else more private. Each time, I had the urge to smack them. Each time, he had nudged my leg with his as they ran their fingers through his hair and whispered sweet nothings in his ear. He politely rejected all of them.

I admired him for his patience, and he did have a point, given that we were still nurturing an alliance with the succubi. And it wasn't like I had any claim over Draven, despite what the first succubus had said. Still, I didn't feel comfortable leaving him in the company of horny warrior chicks.

Nevertheless, as I watched a seventh—or eighth?—succubus approach us, swaying her hips to the beat of the drums, I decided enough was enough. Draven casually chewed on what looked like small purple berries, popping them into his mouth one at a time. A smirk tugged at the corner of his mouth as his nostrils flared.

"I think there's another one coming our way," he mused, sniffing the air. He seemed amused, which only added more wood to the fire of my internal struggle.

"I think it's time we take you to bed now," I replied with a faux-friendly tone, as if announcing the weather during a news segment on TV.

"I think you're right."

I didn't expect that. I'd figured he'd contradict me, purely by instinct. We'd become experts at butting heads. But I welcomed his approval and quickly stood up. I took his hand, and he rose to his feet with a wobble. My hands automatically gripped his arms, and he stilled, his body barely an inch from mine.

My mind was fuzzy from all the amplified sounds and scents around me, but I managed to give the approaching succubus a sideways glance; she'd stopped and was watching us intently, her sapphire eyes narrowed into thin lines.

"You smell good," Draven muttered to me under his breath, his chest rising with each deep breath he took.

My cheeks heated, but my mind tried to take a rational approach. He wasn't very steady on his feet, and he was oversharing. The succubi were definitely having an effect on the Druid, and something told me the rose potion had played a part in this.

"Yeah, we definitely need to take you to bed," I replied bluntly and walked him toward one of the tents that had been prepared for us.

He went in first, and I looked over my shoulder to see the succubus still standing there, watching us. I quickly followed Draven inside and pulled the large fur cover over the entrance.

A lamp had been lit and set on a metal box in the middle. Layer upon layer of animal skins and soft furs formed the most comfortable floor I had ever seen. I quickly moved around Draven, despite my own mild lightheadedness, and pulled a few pillows and furs into one spot to fashion a makeshift bed.

I then took Draven by his hand and helped him lie down, as he still wasn't very steady. He was heavier than I remembered, and I lost my grip on him. He landed with a thud and laughed, leaving me embarrassed and befuddled.

"What's so funny?" I croaked while he took off his boots and lay on his back, his head resting against a few pillows.

"The effect that these succubi have on us. I've never been so close to one…to so many, for that matter, in my entire life," he replied.

I sat down next to him and removed my own boots. Only then did I feel the tension in my muscles and realize how badly my feet hurt from the trip. I looked over to Draven. He looked relaxed. A smile was imprinted on his face, and his forearm covered the top half of his head.

"You promised you'd tell me more about the sleeping Daughter," I gently reminded him. I realized that his current state of mind might help him answer some of my questions about her.

He shushed me, bringing a finger to his lips.

"Don't mention her here," he whispered. "No other creature in this area can know about her existence. She's extremely fragile while still in her egg. We can't risk anyone finding out."

"But the succubi are helping us," I replied, frowning.

"The succubi are helping themselves, and we are useful to them. Just like we are helping ourselves, and they are useful to us. Don't be fooled, Serena. This is still war, and these are still political alliances. They can't know about her for now. Once she awakens, it won't matter anymore."

"Why won't it matter?"

"I get the feeling that the Daughters were right. She may be our secret weapon against Azazel, so we can't reveal her existence to anyone. It's part of the pact I made with them when she first appeared, and they brought her to me." His voice was low.

"Where did she come from?"

"Where they all came from. The top of Mount Agrith, the tallest mountain of Eritopia. But she was found much, much later. Shortly after I was born, to be precise. Which was strange but, since we don't know who lays these eggs, all we can do is guess."

"The Daughters really don't know?"

"No, they do not. Now enough with the questions, Serena. I told you it's not safe to talk about this here," he quietly reprimanded me.

I let out a breath and lay down next to him, my lips pursed while I stared at the ceiling. A huge, coffee-colored animal hide stretched neatly over the thick wooden skeleton of the tent. I couldn't help but wonder what creature it came from. It was enormous.

"In the meantime, however, we need to get more out of the Oracles," Draven said, breaking the silence that had briefly settled between us. "Their visions hold the key to stopping Azazel's bloodbath before we bring out the sleeping nightmare…"

"I'm well aware of that," I replied and instantly thought of Phoenix, lying in that bed in the basement back at the mansion, unconscious and helpless. I thought of Aida and Vita as well, unwilling participants in a game in which only Azazel and Draven seemed to know all the rules.

Draven must have sensed the change in my demeanor as I thought of my brother. His hand settled gently over mine, and my breath faltered.

"He'll be okay, Serena. I assure you. The herbs we gave him have awakened others from far more dangerous states." His voice was soothing, resonating in my chest. His fingers brushed up the length of my forearm, igniting my skin inch by inch.

I pulled my arm away and rolled over to the side, my back to him. I took deep breaths and closed my eyes, trying to regain some form of control over my senses. The rose drink still lingered in my bloodstream, making me hear and smell everything that was so fascinating about him—his heartbeat, the scent of musk—and midnight in the forest. I needed to keep a clear head with Draven still recovering from the succubi's influence.

But I didn't get to relax for long. He rolled over to his side shortly afterward, and spooned me into a tight embrace. His arms snaked around my waist and pulled me into him, and I felt his body heat melt into mine.

I stiffened. I opened my mouth to say something, but words didn't want to come out.

"Just go to sleep." He dug his face into my hair, quieting my protest.

I felt his breath on the back of my neck, a sublime reminder of the previous night, before the Destroyers. It warmed my skin and spread throughout my body, ultimately softening every muscle and every bone that I had.

Lying there in his arms, I closed my eyes. His breath continued to warm me, and my spine disintegrated one vertebra at a time.

I wanted to stay awake for longer lingering in the feeling of him, yet a deep sleep snuck up on me and robbed me of my consciousness. But it was okay, because I was in Draven's arms.

Phoenix
[HAZEL & TEJUS'S SON]

I need to see her.

I woke up in the basement. I sat up and looked around. I was in one of the beds. Aida and Field were asleep on the floor beneath me.

The lights were dim, barely flickering in two oil lamps on the other side of the chamber. I couldn't feel much. No pain. Just the urge to see *her*. Nothing else.

My mind was devoid of any other thought.

I felt something cold under my hand. I picked it up. It was the stone knife that the Daughters had given me, the twine around its handle smudged with dried blood. I thought I'd dropped it in the swamp during my tackle with the shape-shifters.

I remembered everything. Sparring with Jovi. Hearing the shrills. Seeing two succubi get torn to shreds by shape-shifters in the jungle beyond the protective shield. Their blood like mercury sprayed against the trees as the monsters killed them. A third succubi running out and falling into the swamp. Jovi rushing to help her. Me jumping in to distract the shape-shifters while Jovi tried to get her out of there.

My feet getting knocked off the ground. The knife leaving my hand in the fall.

Then the darkness.

My dream of her. Of us.

I looked at the knife again.

The Daughters must have returned it to me. I had a job to do.

I need to see her.

I got off the bed, careful not to wake Aida or Field. I walked toward the stairs, my steps silent on the cold floor. My body moved faster than my thoughts. I went outside.

My mind was a blur.

I looked up to find the indigo sky speckled with a myriad of stars. My feet took me into the garden, to the magnolia tree.

Her tree.

I need to see her. I need to help her.

Vita
[Grace and Lawrence's daughter]

I had spent most of the afternoon practicing my newly-awakened fae abilities. There had been so much joy and energy flowing through me that I felt it would have been a pity to let that go to waste. I had to harness what I'd brought to the surface. I needed my fae strength for what waited ahead for me, for us.

Being an Oracle felt like a horrible fate if I couldn't do anything to stop the horrific future that I had seen in my first visions. Developing my fae power had given me a newfound sense of strength. The self-confidence that flowed through me made it easier for me to manipulate the candle flames.

I was so entranced by what I could do, I'd forgotten to take any breaks.

I must have dozed off at some point. I woke up under the magnolia tree to the midnight breeze rustling through the grass. The sky above was a dark, almost black blue, speckled with stars. The temperature had dropped significantly, sending shivers down my spine.

It was quiet around me, except for the cicadas chirping in the distance. I sat up and rubbed my hands over my face. I was shaking from the cold, and my skin was like ice. I rose to my feet and stretched my arms out, ready to continue my sleep in my bed upstairs under a dozen blankets.

I turned to walk toward the house and stopped as Phoenix walked out.

My eyes grew wide, and my chest inflated with the pure delight of seeing him up and about.

"Phoenix! You're awake!" I exclaimed and took a few steps forward. I intended to hug him, but something was off, and I stilled. He kept walking toward me, and I noticed something in his hand.

"Phoenix, are you okay?"

He didn't answer. His face was devoid of any expression, his eyes half-closed.

He stopped in front of the magnolia tree, just a few yards away from me. I looked at him, but he completely ignored me, staring blankly ahead.

His hand came forward, and I got a better look at what he was holding—a strange-looking knife with a long blade made of stone. My heart stopped.

"Phoenix, what are you doing?"

He didn't answer.

Panic surged through me. This wasn't right.

Phoenix drove the knife into his chest. It happened so quickly that I barely registered the movement.

I froze. It went all the way in. Blood spurted from the wound, trickling down his shirt and into the ground.

I couldn't move. I couldn't react. I couldn't believe what I was seeing.

My mouth opened, but no sound came out.

Phoenix's expression was blank, as if he didn't feel anything.

Blood poured and seeped into the dirt at his feet.

Maybe a minute passed.

Then the ground cracked open beneath Phoenix. Thick roots shot up, swirling frantically. They tangled around his body like hungry snakes, crackling as they tightened their hold on him and pulled him into the ground.

The earth swallowed him whole and closed itself up like nothing had happened. He just vanished into the grass. Gone without a trace. A layer of grass spread quietly above.

And then I screamed.

It was as if time had resumed its flow. I regained control over my body and my senses. I screamed from the bottom of my lungs. I screamed after Phoenix, I screamed at the sight of him stabbing himself in the chest, I screamed at his unnatural disappearance.

My shrieks pierced the night.

AidA
[Victoria & Bastien's daughter]

The floor felt cold beneath me. I woke up, realizing that I'd fallen asleep on the floor in the basement. Field and I had been sitting there all afternoon, our backs against the bed frame, talking.

I rolled over on my back and yawned, then looked to my right. Field slept next to me.

A dim light danced in the darkness, just enough for me to take in his every feature. I was dangerously close to him, his face barely an inch away from mine. It was one of those rare opportunities when I could look at him completely undisturbed.

He looked so peaceful in his sleep. His features were smooth with a few rebellious strands of black hair falling over his face. My mouth turned into a smile. A deep sigh rolled from my chest. His beauty overwhelmed me.

Field opened his eyes to look right into mine.

I froze, staring into two turquoise gems, shadowed by long, black eyelashes.

My words jammed in my throat, my heart thumped against my ribs, and I had no control over my body. The way he looked at me was different, darker and more intense than anything I had ever seen coming from him.

We stayed like that for several moments. I didn't know what to do, so I just lay there, worried that I'd ruin it somehow. I'd grown so accustomed to being the little half-wolf girl that he barely paid attention to that I didn't know what to make of him now when he saw me for myself.

His eyes drilled hot holes into my soul, his face so close to mine that I could feel myself burning up from the proximity.

I'd spent so much time fantasizing about a moment like this and yet had no idea how to react to it in real life. This was real life. Field drew his face closer to mine, enough for me to feel his breath brush over my lips, igniting fires deep in my core. I couldn't move. I couldn't breathe.

I parted my lips instinctively. A singular thought nibbled at the back of my mind: *What if he comes closer?*

His gaze dropped to my mouth. His tongue flicked over his

lower lip. Shadows passed over his eyes, like millions of thoughts colliding as his lips came dangerously close to mine. Barely an inch was left between us when his eyes searched and found mine again.

His eyebrows sank into a subtle frown, his teeth sinking into his lip.

My pulse reverberated in my ears, my mind begging him to close the distance.

A sharp scream pierced the silence.

The moment between us dissipated. Vita's strident wail reverberated from outside. We both shot to our feet, staring at each other with wide eyes.

Another scream echoed into the basement, and my blood froze.

SERENA
[HAZEL AND TEJUS'S DAUGHTER]

I dreamed about Draven that night. We were sitting by the bonfire with dozens of succubi surrounding us asking him to join them in their tents. Destroyers sat atop winged horses, flying overhead, circling above the camp. They couldn't get in. My subconscious had mixed some facts together, between the swamp witches' illusion spell and the mansion's protective shield. All I could think of was getting Draven out of there, unsure of what I feared more: the succubi or the Destroyers.

I opened my eyes, enveloped in blissful warmth and my face mere inches from Draven's as I lay in his embrace beneath a beige animal fur. It felt so good, so *right*. Morning light peeked through the tent's loose seams, coming down in thin white beams.

His hair was tousled over his forehead, and his breathing was even. His frame made me feel tiny in his arms. I took in every feature of his, every edge, and every line that made him who he was. I clasped my hands to my chest, unable to move in the absence of space between us. My body molded against his, my soft figure melting into him like butter in a hot pan.

I turned my palms and flattened them on his broad chest, my fingers splayed across the linen shirt. I could feel the rune marks beneath my fingertips. His wounds were still healing after our difficult meeting with the Daughters of Eritopia.

The world around us was quiet and distant as I listened to his breathing. I could stay there forever. How had he managed to sneak into my soul like this?

"How did you become so important to me?" I whispered, feeling the need to let those words out while he slept.

He didn't move.

I sighed and gently brushed my fingers against his chin, careful not to wake him up. His skin was as soft as I remembered it. Even asleep, he sent waves of buzzing energy through my entire body and heated up my core.

"I wish I could look straight into your soul and understand what goes on in your head." My voice was so low it was barely audible. "Wish I knew how you felt…"

His lips stretched into a lazy smile, and I froze. My cheeks flamed. He'd heard.

Panic locked into my muscles. *You and your big damn mouth, Serena!*

He let out a deep breath and tightened his hold on me, somehow pulling me even closer to him. Another inch and our bodies would fuse into each other. The air left my lungs and, as I drew more in, I felt my chest rise and push into his.

Draven's smile faded, and a muscle tensed in his jaw. His fingers spread out on my back, trailing along my spine. I felt them move up, reaching the area between my shoulder blades. His touch sent shivers through my entire being, heedless of my shirt's fabric.

His lips transfixed me as they parted slowly. His heart drummed against me, echoing into my ribcage. His breathing accelerated, heating me up with each exhalation of hot air over my face.

My instinct took over, and I abandoned myself in his arms, relaxing completely. My every curve rested against his rock hard body, while his hands continued tracing imaginary lines on my back. The bottom of my shirt lifted slowly, and his fingers found my skin beneath.

We both stopped breathing and stilled for a second. Then, his mouth came over mine and locked me in an ardent kiss. His lips pressed against mine while his fingers slipped upward underneath my shirt, exploring further, leaving traces of fire wherever he touched me.

I burned in his arms as he deepened the kiss. His tongue melted with mine. I felt him open up inside my head, coaxing my inner-sentry to dive into his very soul. I allowed myself to expand my mind into his, and, much to my surprise, he let me in.

My eyes closed as our kiss grew hungrier and our mouths devoured each other. His fingers gently dug into my skin. He let me in, and a river of images washed over me. I held his face and drew him even deeper.

I saw him running after Elissa, laughing and tumbling in the gardens outside. I saw his father coming home from a journey as Draven ran into his arms. I saw him roaming around the house on his own in loneliness and despair. I saw Elissa ending her own life as he watched her through the fire. The pain pierced me, and I felt what he'd felt at that moment.

I wanted to cry out, tears stinging my eyes, but Draven didn't let go of me. He allowed me to go deeper, his mouth consuming mine. I forgot to breathe.

I saw myself through his eyes back at the mansion, shouting at him furiously, then in his arms, tight against his chest as he rescued me from the shape-shifters. I saw myself crying as I watched him go blind, as darkness covered everything. My heart expanded as a golden light glazed me in something so intense I felt like I was going to explode. And I welcomed everything.

Draven gave me so much in that long, feverish kiss. His memories, his thoughts, his feelings. All that gold, all that brightness—it was all channeled at me. It was meant for me, and I took it happily. I welcomed the heat seeping into my mind and spreading through my chest and my limbs. I wrapped my arms around his neck and moaned into the kiss, pulling myself even harder into his embrace.

His arms tightened around me, a feat I had thought impossible, and we dove deeper, lips crushing as we consumed one another. I ran my fingers through his hair. He pulled himself away, just enough for us to take a deep breath before he took me on another rapturous journey, never breaking the mind-meld. He kissed me again, and I responded with everything I had.

"The scouts are back!"

Bijarki's voice crashed down on us from just outside the tent.

The reality of that sentence broke everything down. It ended the kiss. We pulled away, both of us trying to recover our breath and our senses. The real world tumbled back into view so fast and unforgiving that neither of us had enough time to properly digest what had just happened.

I stood up and helped Draven to his feet. His face sought mine. His jagged breathing mirrored mine. His lips were red and slightly swollen. His tongue flicked over them.

Bijarki's head popped into the tent, and his jaw dropped

when he saw us. I had a feeling both Draven and I looked exactly how I felt—flushed and ruffled, awkwardly wobbling on our feet.

"The scouts are coming back," his flat tone drilled into me.

"Yeah, we're coming out now," I managed to say. I ran my fingers through my hair for a quick detangle.

Draven was quiet, his jaw tense and lips firmly closed.

I walked out of the tent, and he followed quietly behind me.

Bijarki waited for us outside and took his time to measure us from head to toe.

My cheeks still burned. None of us said anything for a few moments until Bijarki pointed at the far end of the camp, where a small stone bridge reached out over a clear stream into the jungle, beyond the invisible barrier. He walked toward it, and Draven and I followed quietly behind.

A few moments later, Draven placed his hand on my shoulder, his fingers gently pressing into my flesh and sending another heatwave through me.

"Is this normal?" he asked, his voice low and husky.

"What—is what normal?" I stuttered, still trying to regain control over my senses.

"The awkward silence. I've never been so close to anyone before in my life. I don't know how things work in this situation. Nor do I know how to behave or what to do next." His confession threw hammers into my stomach.

He had a point, though. I didn't know how to respond to all of this either. I had never been so close to anyone. I'd read plenty of books, but none had really prepared me for the real thing. I stopped and turned to face him, my palm flat on his chest. His heart thudded beneath.

"I don't know either, Draven. This is new to both of us," I managed to say and bit into my lower lip. I could still taste his kiss.

He smiled radiantly, took my hand, and we moved toward the bridge, our fingers intertwined.

"Let's not make it awkward then," he retorted.

All I could do was smile and hold on.

JOVI
[VICTORIA & BASTIEN'S SON]

I woke up with a pounding headache. My eyes felt sore in their sockets as I slowly regained consciousness from a very deep sleep. I couldn't even remember dreaming. My whole body throbbed, like I'd fallen down a flight of stairs. Repeatedly.

What the hell happened last night?

That internal question swiftly triggered a dazzling array of memories. I sat up and checked my surroundings. I was inside one of the tents that the succubi had raised for us, resting on top of soft animal furs and pillows.

The succubi…

The previous night's feast flashed before my eyes—the

strange savory preparations, the sweet kind-of plums, the spicy rose drink in golden pitchers that I kept gulping down like water...

Oh. The drink.

Then came the memories of the giant bonfire's flames licking at the sky with a plethora of sparks crackling upwards into a column of smoke, the tribal drums beating frenetically as scantily dressed succubi danced and swayed their voluptuous hips to the rhythm, Anjani talking to Hansa on the other side of the fire, beautiful young succubi trying to seduce me, and Anjani claiming me.

She claimed me!

I looked over to my right and found her sleeping next to me, curled up beneath a light brown blanket stitched from animal hides. Sunshine pierced through the tent's seams, and one ray of light landed directly on her face. Her skin shimmered in it. Her chest rose with each breath.

I remembered her tormented words from last night—her insecurities about me, the frustration over her succubus nature, and the way it affected people around her. She'd been so reserved around me, afraid she'd influence my behavior toward her. When I'd run my fingers through her hair, she had lit up like a star and then questioned the authenticity of my gesture. She'd feared it was her succubus effect rather than my own intent.

I'd been too drowsy to object. The spicy rose drink had

enhanced my senses to incredible new levels, while the entire succubi tribe had projected their desires on me. I had been pretty out of it. Looking back now, fully awake and in possession of a migraine, I was pretty sure I had meant what I'd said to her.

I had told her I liked her.

What was I thinking?

Clearly I hadn't been thinking.

What's done is done.

I took a breath of resolve. I looked at Anjani again, sleeping peacefully next to me. I lay back on my side, drawing myself close to her.

I decided to enjoy the view for as long as I had. I took in her every curve, every inch of glimmering skin, full lips that begged to be kissed, the thin blade of her nose. My insides burned at the sight of it all. My breath was ragged, and I felt myself biting the inside of my cheek, unable to take my eyes off her.

And then it hit me. She was sleeping. There was no way she was working any succubus charms on me while sleeping. That meant everything I felt in that moment was very much real and very much my own doing.

I was attracted to a succubus I barely knew anything about, and what I knew belonged in a book on wartime brutality in indigenous tribes. She was the heir to an entire clan of warrior females expected to treat men like chunks of meat with simple and limited uses. Yet she had expressed a desire to be genuinely liked by someone.

By me.

My fingers found a solitary strand of her black hair, reaching out to me on the blanket between us. I played with it, letting it curl around my index finger as I listened to the sound of her breathing.

Slowly but surely I found a new objective. I would explore this further. I would see where it took me. I would ride this wave with her until she gave in to me.

I moved in just enough to feel her breath on my face.

She's perfect.

Her eyes opened wide. Her breathing stopped. I could hear her heart as it started drumming in her chest. I almost lost myself in those infinite pools of emerald green and golden flakes as her pupils dilated. Her lips parted slowly and, for a brief moment, I wondered what would happen if I kissed her.

She didn't give me a chance.

She pushed me back, her palms slamming into my chest with considerable force. I slid backwards on my side, and the air was knocked out of my lungs.

Anjani shot to her feet so quickly, I didn't fully register the movement. She stared at me, speechless and glowing again like I'd seen her do last night. Then, she ran out.

It took me a few deep breaths to recover. I stood up and rubbed my hands all over my face, pleased to see my resolve was still there. I would get to her. One way or another, she would open up to me.

* * *

I stepped outside after I changed my clothes and quickly washed my face in the little basin that had been left there for me by our hosts.

Morning unraveled gently over the mountains, dressing everything in a pinkish hue. The trill of birds and murmur of cold springs running freely put a smile on my face. The sun rose big and bright as if encouraging me to keep going.

My chest swelled with optimism, and I watched the succubi prepare for the day— some going about their chores, others sharpening their swords and lacing their arrows with poison for a shape-shifter hunt, and some washing clothes in the stream.

"Hope you slept well." Hansa saluted me, and her palm landed heavily on my shoulder.

"I did, I did, thank you," I replied, smiling.

"Let's go to the bridge on the other side. The scouts are coming back."

She didn't wait for me to answer. Instead, her arm on my shoulder pulled me in that direction. It felt awkward, like she was crushing my masculinity. She was a seasoned warrior, and I was still technically a puppy.

Halfway through our walk to the bridge, I decided to ask

about Anjani's glow. It fascinated me the way she'd literally flared up.

"Why do succubi glow?"

"You mean our skin color?" Hansa frowned, confused by my poorly composed question.

"No, no. I mean really glow. Not your usual shimmer. I saw Anjani light up like the moon last night. I've never seen that before."

Hansa laughed all the way to the foot of the bridge, where we met Draven, Serena, and Bijarki, who already awaited the scouts' return.

"You saw her blush, which is quite rare. Tell me later how you managed to do that," Hansa quickly explained and dismissed me with a slap on the shoulder.

She turned to speak to Draven, and I was left with more questions than answers.

Serena and I greeted each other.

Anjani joined us. "The scouts were seen by our guards earlier, coming in from the southwest," she explained and pointed at a slim tower fifty feet east of the bridge.

It was a simple construction, made of solid wood and large palm leaves that served as a roof. It was occupied by two succubi with crossbows. We'd come in from the other side of the camp yesterday, and I hadn't paid much attention to this side of the settlement. Nevertheless, it told me that the succubi were always on their guard, always keeping an eye out over the jungle.

I looked at Anjani, but she avoided my gaze, focusing on Serena instead. Hansa's words rolled through my head. I had made her *blush*. I felt a self-satisfied smirk lifting the corners of my mouth, but the sound of hooves broke my line of thought and made us all turn our heads toward the bridge.

The jungle fanned out beyond the stream in its dark hues of green and purple, its foliage dense with thick shrubs. The leaves rustled as a large figure emerged from the depths of the wild forest. We watched quietly as one horse stepped into the clearing, followed by two more.

There was something wrong with this image.

Anjani gasped.

The horses had returned, but the scouts—the three succubi I'd seen yesterday— were slumped over. Long arrows had been lodged in their backs and sides, up to six each.

"NO!" Hansa shouted, her voice thundering across the entire camp and echoing into the forest.

The three black stallions clamored over the bridge, neighing and shaking their heads. Hansa, Anjani, and Bijarki grabbed the reins of each horse and pulled them into camp. Serena stood by Draven's side, her eyes wide with horror. She mumbled something to Draven. I figured she was describing what she was seeing.

"No, my sisters, no!" Hansa's voice trembled as she pulled

Kalli from her horse.

Her body slumped on the ground covered in silver blood. Her shimmer was gone, her skin pale and nearly transparent. Hansa knelt in front of her and pulled the arrows out, cursing under her breath. My stomach churned at the sight.

A few feet over, Anjani pulled Thenna's body down, laying it on the grass. She hadn't made it either. Tears ran down Anjani's face, her lips trembling as she whispered something into the dead succubus's ear. She dropped a gentle kiss on her forehead before she removed the arrows.

We heard Riga moan as Bijarki lifted her off the horse and laid her down. I darted over to them, landing on my knees next to her. I ripped off a large piece of my shirt and pressed it against her stomach where an arrow poked out. She had been hit from different angles.

Riga coughed, her glimmer dimming as she struggled to keep her eyes open. Her lips and chin were glazed in silver blood. Anjani and Hansa rushed over to help.

"We need help here!" Hansa shouted over her shoulder to the succubi washing clothes in the stream.

The young ones ran off to one of the nearby tents while the others sounded the alarm, a loud guttural shrill from horn-shaped instruments I had never heard before.

Soon enough, we were surrounded by the entire tribe.

Serena and Draven stood helplessly to the side.

I kept the pressure on Riga's wounds while Anjani slipped her legs under so she could rest the scout's head on her thighs. She gently caressed her face.

"You'll be okay, Riga, we've got you," she said, her voice trembling.

"Who did this to you, sister? What happened?" Hansa barked.

Another succubus pushed Bijarki away and pulled out rolls of white linen and several flasks of dark blue liquid. She poured it onto the linen rolls and applied one to each arrow wound without removing the projectile. She gave me one to place on the wound I had been covering, and I followed her lead.

"It should stop the bleeding before we can pull the arrows out," the succubus said. She pressed against a hip wound, making Riga moan and cough.

"They have a message," the scout managed to say between coughs. She tried to inhale but instead wheezed and spit out more blood.

"Who? What happened?" Hansa insisted, trying to keep Riga's focus on her.

"Arid... They joined Azazel's army..."

The realization crashed into us like a devastating wave. My throat burned, and my inner-wolf growled beneath my skin. Anger flowed through me, incandescent and unforgiving.

"They...they warned us to leave before the Destroyers

returned to their camp," Riga continued, struggling to speak. "But we tried to convince them to meet with you…"

"They refused," Hansa concluded and cursed under her breath.

"The Destroyers returned and…and shot their arrows… They said you're next," Riga managed to say. She started choking on her own silver blood.

Bijarki pulled me away as the succubus nurse and Anjani rolled Riga on her side, trying to ease her breathing. Hansa sighed and stood up, rubbing her face with her palms.

"It's too late," she said to the nurse. "Those are Destroyer arrows. She will die."

Anjani looked down at Riga as her body started convulsing. White foam spewed out of her mouth.

"No, no, there must be something we can do!" Anjani shouted, watching helplessly as Riga choked and writhed in pain.

"There's nothing we can do!" Hansa shouted back. "End it!"

Anjani froze, her eyes wide open. The succubus nurse pulled out a knife and slit Riga's throat in one swift move and immediately covered her head with a cloth so none of us could see the end of it.

I groaned, and Bijarki hissed next to me. I then remembered he'd seen this before. He'd done what the nurse had done too, to his friend Kristos, whose father had betrayed him and betrayed us all.

Hansa left our side, fury emanating from her like a blazing fire. Anjani fell backward and swallowed her tears as she looked at her hands, covered in silver blood. She seemed hazy, as if in a state of shock. I reached out to her. I wanted to comfort her and take her away from there, but Bijarki pulled me in the opposite direction. We went after Hansa.

I looked over my shoulder and saw Serena and Draven following us, their faces stern and dark.

SERENA
[HAZEL AND TEJUS'S DAUGHTER]

Everything was happening too fast. Our hopes of forging an alliance with Kristos's father had come crashing down in flames, instead giving us three dead bodies and the promise that we would be next.

I held Draven's hand as we walked away from the scouts. My stomach threatened to expel everything I had eaten the previous night at the sight of their dead bodies. I couldn't be there for another second.

We followed Bijarki, Jovi, and Hansa as they rushed toward the bonfire.

"We have to do something!" the incubus shouted after

Hansa, who turned to face him, her nostrils flaring and teeth bared.

"You're damn right we'll do something! We're going to war!" Hansa roared so that the entire tribe could hear.

"That's not what I had in mind," Bijarki muttered.

"No one cares what you've got in mind! We are going to war!"

One by one, the succubi gathered around us, grumbling and hissing.

They were all furious, clutching their weapons and moving their weight from one leg to another like the restless warriors they all were.

The fire licked at the clear sky next to us. The wood crackled and spit out black smoke and sparks.

"That would be foolish," Draven said, his hand over mine.

"That was a declaration of war," Hansa pointed at the bridge behind us. "We do not cower in front of these snakes! We kill snakes!"

"Five thousand incubi just joined Azazel's ranks. Don't let rage get the better of you, Hansa. You still have your weapons, and we still have the Oracles." Draven raised his voice enough to temper the groans and hisses oozing from the crowd.

"They killed our sisters!" Hansa shouted back. She swallowed back tears.

That was a rare sight. I hadn't known Hansa for long, but she struck me as a ruthless warrior. It turned out that she, too, was capable of grief, and I felt sympathy for her and for Anjani, who silently joined me as we watched the increasingly heated exchange between her sister and Draven.

"You'll just get yourselves killed if you go after the Destroyers now, with or without your dragon tears. They will rip you to shreds, and deep down, you know it!" The Druid held his ground, unwilling to let our newfound allies march into certain death.

Hansa paced back and forth for a few moments, her jaw clenched and a vein throbbing against her forehead. Her left hand gripped the hilt of her sword, knuckles white.

Jovi stood between Draven and Bijarki to my left. He occasionally threw glances at Anjani to my right. Concern drew a frown on his face, and he took a step forward.

"My sister is one of the Oracles, Hansa. I don't want to diminish her chances of survival in this world by losing you and your tribe to Azazel," he said, his voice firm and his chin high.

Hansa stilled and stared at him. The seconds stretched long. Then she took a deep breath and dropped her shoulders.

"What do you suggest we do then, Druid?" she hissed.

"We use a strategic approach," he replied. "We collect intelligence on Azazel and the movements of his Destroyers through our Oracles. You send out scouts to reach out to all the other remaining factions still standing in the jungles of Eritopia."

"Most of the incubi have already joined Azazel," Bijarki interjected, running a hand through his hair. He'd seen all this before. He'd been through all this before. The pain of betrayal still marred his otherwise beautiful features.

"I'm not talking about the incubi here," Draven said.

"Then who are you talking about?" Hansa shot back, losing her patience.

"The Dearghs, the Sluaghs, the Lamias... All the other creatures that call Eritopia their home, as savage as they may be. They're threatened by Azazel too. Just because he's targeting the incubi now doesn't mean he won't come after them later."

"They're wildlings, Druid. They don't make alliances!"

"Then persuade them! And if you can't persuade them, seduce them! You're natural born seductresses, after all. There's nothing you can't do if you set your minds to it!" Draven replied. "We need them all to join us. If we can't get the incubi to fight, we get the others. There is a war coming, and we need the numbers."

I listened to his impassioned speech. His hand still clutched mine. Our fingers intertwined, and I felt the determination pouring out of him and into my body. I could've sworn he was opening up to me further, letting me feel what he felt—hope, despite everything that had just happened.

Hansa took some time to deliberate, looking around the camp until her eyes settled on Anjani. Her gaze softened at the sight of her sister, and the slightest smile passed over her face.

"Why would they want to help us? Why would they want to fight alongside us?" Hansa asked Draven.

"You mean, besides the survival of their species?"

"You don't know them, Druid. You've been stuck in that mansion of yours for too long." Hansa smirked. "Most of them live out there in the jungle with no use to Azazel whatsoever. We need more than some bombs and Oracles to spark their interest. The Dearghs and the Sluaghs believe that whatever happens in Eritopia is the will of the Daughters, for example. How will you convince them to go against that?"

A moment passed before Draven answered.

"We have the last Daughter of Eritopia."

Many jaws dropped once he said that, including mine. He'd been so adamant about keeping this a secret. What was he thinking?

Hansa's eyes grew wide, and she tipped her head to one side. "What did you just say?"

"I said we have the last Daughter of Eritopia. Her sisters entrusted me to look after her until she awakens. I'm pretty sure the Dearghs and Sluaghs will wish to serve someone who has the Daughters' favor. *And* the last Daughter, on top of that," Draven continued, his confidence bolstered.

"How did that come to happen?" Hansa asked with sheer fascination.

"We made a deal in exchange for my mansion's protection. The safety of the Oracle in my home in return for the safety of their sister. We need to gather all forces available and strike Azazel, Hansa. The last Daughter may awaken, like her sisters have predicted, and play her part in this, or she may not. We don't know for sure. But we can't shy away from this fight. We have to come together and give it our best shot regardless. Eritopia belongs to all of us."

Seconds ticked by before Hansa replied. I figured she was going through all possible scenarios in her head. And, like all of my previous musings, she arrived at the same conclusion—all roads led to the sleeping Daughter, one way or another.

"So it shall be, then," she said with newfound calm. "I will send my sisters out to find the wildlings and broker alliances."

A sigh gusted from my chest, relieved to see them agree on this. Draven nodded and tightened his grip on my hand.

"We will return to the mansion and work with our Oracles to gain insight on Azazel, then."

Jovi, Bijarki, and I looked at each other and nodded. We had our work cut out for us since Phoenix, Aida, and Vita were still very new at this Oracle stuff and hadn't fully developed their abilities. Draven seemed to have deliberately omitted that little fact from Hansa, but I couldn't blame him. We had to sort of fake it to make it. But there was a common sense of determination between us. We'd all give it our best shot and support the Oracles.

I was eager to return to the safety of the protective shield while the rest of the pieces arranged themselves on the chessboard. Hansa snapped her fingers and called out to her generals.

Three women as tall and imposing as Hansa stepped forward from the crowd clad in metal plates and black leather. They'd painted vertical crimson stripes on their faces, and long heavy swords hung from their belts.

Hansa instructed them to form search parties and spread out to find the Dearghs, the Sluaghs, and the elusive Lamias far south, whatever those species even were. Anjani didn't move. Her arms were wrapped around her torso, and she stared at the ground.

"We'll be going soon, then," Draven said to Hansa. "We have a day and a half ahead of us for the journey. We need to take advantage of the daylight."

Hansa dismissed her generals. The succubi scattered, each preparing for their assignments. She came up to us and placed a hand on Anjani's shoulder, startling her back into the conversation.

"That's nonsense," Hansa grinned. "I'm not letting you risk the long journey back."

"Unless you have a better way, we'll have to. My vision impairment won't let me use my travel runes," Draven replied.

"But I *do* have a better way. Follow me."

* * *

Hansa took us to her tent, the biggest in the camp. It was covered in massive black furs. The interior was dressed in layers of semi-transparent fabrics in shades of red and white, the complete visual opposite of the menacing exterior.

I walked in first with Draven, followed by Jovi, Bijarki, and Anjani.

At the far end was a slab of what looked like obsidian—a smooth, black crystal as tall as she was. She walked up to it and turned around to face us.

"This was given to me as a gift from a Druid once. Many moons ago, before Azazel went mad and started slaughtering his own kind," Hansa briefly explained.

I whispered to Draven, describing the black crystal. He straightened his back, recognizing the object from its description.

"You have a passage stone?" he asked, his voice pitched with surprise.

"What's a passage stone?" Anjani asked, staring at the obsidian.

Judging by the perplexed look on her face, she hadn't known her sister had it.

"It's extremely powerful magic from the Druids, thought to

be extinct," Draven explained. "I still have one back at the mansion, but I never use it, because it needs another to connect with. I didn't know there were any left!"

"Anjani, you didn't know about this?" I asked her, and she shook her head in response.

"Little sisters don't know everything." Hansa grinned. "I was going to tell her once she advanced through our ranks a little further. The passage stone is a well-guarded secret. Only I know about it. Well, now you know too."

"What does it do?" I still wasn't clear on its purpose.

"It takes you to wherever there's another passage stone—provided you know your destination, of course. Otherwise you might not like where you end up," Hansa replied.

"This only works if there's another stone on the other side. How did you know I had one?" Draven asked.

"I'm no fool, Druid. You don't strike me as someone who isn't resourceful and cunning. You've been keeping that Daughter to yourself all this time, after all. And besides, Almus had one." Hansa smiled. "Well, he had two. He gave me this one."

I was speechless and, judging by Draven's expression, so was he.

"We'll save that story for another time," Hansa continued. "By the way, Anjani will be joining you."

At the sound of her name, Anjani's eyes grew wide, looking

at each of us with what looked like panic and disapproval. She shook her head.

"No, no, no. Why do I have to go?" She protested.

"Wow, don't get too excited," Jovi shot back, visibly offended.

"It is part of our agreement," Hansa cut them off, her eyes set on Draven. "One of us with you at all times. It's our tradition. Allies are not friends, Druid. We trust no one."

Draven nodded solemnly. "That's perfectly fine with us, if it strengthens our agreement."

"Very well," Hansa concluded. She took out a knife and pulled Draven's hand out. I opened my mouth to protest, but Anjani gripped my arm, her gaze urging me to keep quiet.

"The stone needs the blood of someone who has seen the other stone," the tribe chief said. She sliced his palm.

Draven hissed and tightened his grip on my hand even further, until my bones crackled from the pressure, and I yelped. He instantly relaxed his hold.

Hansa guided his bleeding hand to the stone's surface.

As soon as his blood came in contact with the smooth obsidian, its surface began to ripple, similar to what we had seen the other day before we entered the Red Tribe through the limestone barrier.

"Good. Now it knows where to take you," Hansa said. "Come see us in seven days, Druid. We will have answers by then—good or bad."

Draven nodded and walked through the stone. I followed quietly behind and heard Hansa shout after us as the darkness enveloped me.

"Don't get my sister killed, Druid!"

The warning sent chills down my spine. I held on to Draven's hand, unable to see or hear anything. I could only feel his touch, as we walked through the immaterial blackness. It only lasted a few seconds.

Before I knew it, he'd pulled me out into the dim light of a subterranean chamber. I stumbled into his back.

He held his arms out to stop the others from moving forward. I looked behind and saw an identical slab of obsidian resting against a humid stone wall. Jovi, Anjani, and Bijarki came out of it, one at a time, its surface trembling from the contact before it smoothed itself back to its original state.

We were standing in front of a deep underground pool lit with fluorescent blue water. The pool looked like it had been carved into the stone. We stood on a narrow ridge alongside it, a step from falling into the water.

"This is not the kind of pool you'd want to swim in, believe me," Draven warned.

One by one, we started shuffling toward the end of the ridge, where a narrow staircase had been carved, leading back to the surface of wherever this was.

"What's that smell?" Jovi asked, sniffing the humid air.

I took a deep breath and suddenly felt a little lightheaded. Draven gripped my arm, having heard my inhalation.

"Don't breathe in too much. The water emanates a toxic gas. It was used as an anesthetic by the Druids back in the old days. It's still highly potent. It's mostly odorless, but it will knock you out," Draven explained.

We reached the stairs and climbed up, one by one. We made it to the surface and found ourselves in the back garden of the mansion surrounded by thick rose bushes with the greenhouse to our right.

Vita

[GRACE AND LAWRENCE'S DAUGHTER]

Hours must have passed since I'd seen Phoenix disappear into the ground beneath the magnolia tree, since I'd screamed after him from the bottom of my lungs, since Field and Aida had run outside. I couldn't tell how long I had been there.

I couldn't move. I didn't want to move.

Aida tried to get me away from there to no avail.

My hands dug deep into the grass. Dirt pressed under my fingernails. My eyes stung from the tears that streamed down my face. My throat was parched. My voice was so hoarse I could barely speak.

Field had been trying to dig for hours. He used one of three shovels he'd grabbed from the greenhouse, scooping the black soil, desperately trying to get to where I'd shown him Phoenix had vanished. Every time he went as deep as one yard, the ground rumbled and pushed him out, swelling up with more dirt and filling the hole back up, like nothing had happened.

"It won't let me dig," Field gasped. Beads of sweat rolled down his ashen face.

He kept trying regardless. He dug and cursed every time the earth rejected him. Aida and I used the other shovels to help. Every time we dug in, the tree's roots ejected us. Eventually my legs gave out, and I fell to my knees.

I was exhausted, yet stunned enough to maintain consciousness. Aida collapsed next to me, wiping tears from her face with the back of her hand.

The sun rose over the mansion, drawing pink and blue watercolors across the sky. Bird song traveled on the wind from the surrounding jungle. I couldn't process anything. The image of Phoenix getting tangled into the magnolia tree's roots and vanishing into the ground replayed in my mind, in a torturous loop.

"I don't know what to do," Field said. His dirty palms splayed on his knees as he tried to get his breathing under control.

"What if he's…" Aida's voice trailed off.

Field looked at her with a pained expression.

"He can't be," I heard myself croak. "He—he can't be…"

"What do we do?" She asked without expecting an answer.

None of us had an answer or a reasonable explanation for what had just happened.

The sound of movement in the grass caused us to turn our heads toward the house. Serena came from behind it, holding Draven's hand. Jovi, Bijarki, and Anjani followed. They were back, all in one piece.

"Serena," I gasped.

What was I going to tell her?

How was I going to explain what happened?

No words seemed right to describe what Phoenix had done and how hard we'd tried to reverse it.

She smiled, closing the distance between us.

My heart twisted into knots, and my cheeks burned. Another wave of hot tears poured from my eyes. I watched their expressions change as they approached us.

Serena stopped in front of Field, who stood up and rubbed his sweaty palms against his pants.

"What's wrong?" she asked, anxious.

When no answer came out, she looked around.

None of us spoke.

"Where's Phoenix?" came her second question, the one I dreaded the most.

I felt Aida's arm wrap around my shoulders. I watched Serena's expression change from anxiety to a heart-wrenching frown.

Bijarki took a few steps forward until he reached me. His eyes found mine, but I was sobbing too hard to speak.

"Can somebody please tell me what's going on? Where's my brother?" Serena's voice trembled.

"We fell asleep last night," Field started to explain, his tone low and wavering. "We didn't see him get up and leave…"

Serena's expression lit up.

"He's awake? Where is he?"

"I tried to stop him," I managed to say between sobs, and she looked at me with even more confusion in her blue-green eyes. "I tried…"

"What do you mean?"

"He stopped in front of the tree," Field continued. "He stabbed himself, Serena…"

She gasped, and all color left her face. Her eyes bugged, and her mouth gaped. She lost control over her legs and fell to her knees.

"Serena," Draven said.

She dropped to the ground out of his reach. "Where is he?"

"We… We don't know," Field replied, swallowing back his own tears.

Serena put her hands on the ground, breathing hard from shock. It tore me apart to see her like that. I shuddered in Aida's arms.

"The ground swallowed him," I cried out. "It just opened up, and the magnolia roots shot out and pulled him down. He's down there somewhere!"

"We've been digging for hours," Field said, looking at no one in particular. His hands trembled. "I've been trying to get to him, but the earth won't let me in! It keeps pushing me out! Filling back up! I've been trying for hours!"

Jovi faced Field and clasped his shoulders firmly, trying to calm him down.

Aida held me tightly, as wave after wave of pure devastation crashed into me.

I looked up.

Serena stood up, grabbed one of the shovels, and started digging frantically. But the dirt belched from under her shovel, pushed her back, and filled the hole up again.

Anjani stood still, looking up at the tree.

Bijarki came down on one knee in front of me and lifted my chin with two fingers. His gray eyes stormed into my soul. Another round of tears scorched my eyes. My lips were dry and trembling. The pain on his face seemed to mirror mine. I couldn't take it.

"Phoenix!" Serena screamed into the ground, breaking down in tears. Her sobs tore into me, cutting deep. Raw holes drilled deeper into my chest with every noise she made. She kept shouting after her brother, and none of us could do anything about it.

Draven stood still, an indecipherable expression on his face, his lips pressed tight. He frowned more every time Phoenix's name left Serena's lips.

Bijarki couldn't do anything for me in that moment. We both seemed to know it.

I dropped my head onto Aida's shoulder and waited for…what?

I watched Bijarki from the corner of my eye as he looked up. His face straightened all of a sudden. He stood.

I noticed that Anjani was still staring at the magnolia tree above us. I looked at Bijarki again and watched his eyebrows morph into a puzzled frown as he, too, stared at it.

"Phoenix…" Serena's voice dimmed as she cried, still digging into the merciless dirt.

Jovi kept mumbling words of comfort to Field, who'd drifted into a state of wordless shock.

None of us had been prepared for any of this. None of us knew what to do.

I looked at Anjani, then at Bijarki. They were transfixed by the damn tree.

My gaze followed theirs. My eyes nearly popped out of their sockets as I realized what they were staring at.

The magnolia flowers had turned from their usual pale pink to a vibrant red, the petals swollen and amplifying the size of the tree crown. It was huge and unnatural. It took my breath away.

"What is happening?" I asked.

Aida noticed my consternation and looked up. "What the hell?"

Her mutter drew Field out of his catatonic state. One by one, we all stared up at the red magnolia tree.

"What's going on?" Draven asked.

No one made a sound.

Serena finally looked up with bloodshot eyes. Tears still flowed down her cheeks. She brought a hand up to her mouth to muffle her gasp.

She then turned her attention back to the ground beneath her.

She fell to her knees, looking down, and I saw a glimmer in her eyes as she stared right into the earth, her face just a few inches away.

She was trying to use her True Sight to look for her brother.

"The tree, Draven," Bijarki said, stupefied. "It turned red."

"What?" Draven replied.

"The magnolia blossoms. They're all swollen and red. I've never seen this before in my life," the incubus said.

A moment passed before Draven spoke.

"The tree was given a blood sacrifice," he said, his voice low and cold.

We looked at each other, then at the tree, then back to

Draven. None of us knew what that meant, and no one spoke.

"What's a blood sacrifice?" I finally asked, already fearful of what the answer might be. I swallowed back more tears and leaned against Aida. I felt so weak.

Serena's eyes widened as she continued using her True Sight. She had found something underground and, whatever she'd seen, it had shocked her. Her lips parted, but no sound came out.

Draven's voice shot through the silence:

"It means the last Daughter of Eritopia is about to wake up."

READY FOR MORE?

Dear Shaddict,

Thank you for reading *A Tangle of Hearts*! I hope you enjoyed it.

The next book, **_ASOV 45_** is called **_A Meet of Tribes_**, and it releases **June 15th, 2017**!

Pre-order your copy now and have it delivered automatically on release day — visit: **www.bellaforrest.net**

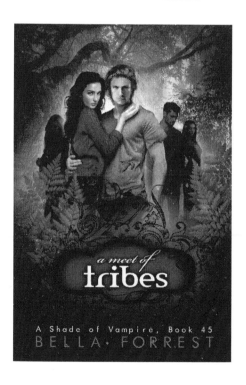

I'll see you on the other side…

Love,
Bella xxx

P.S. Join my VIP email list and I'll send you a personal reminder as soon as I have a new book out. Visit here to sign up: **www.forrestbooks.com** (Your email will be kept 100% private and you can unsubscribe at any time.)

P.P.S. Follow The Shade on Instagram and check out some of the beautiful graphics: @ashadeofvampire

You can also come say hi on Facebook:

www.facebook.com/AShadeOfVampire

And Twitter: @ashadeofvampire

Novak Family Tree

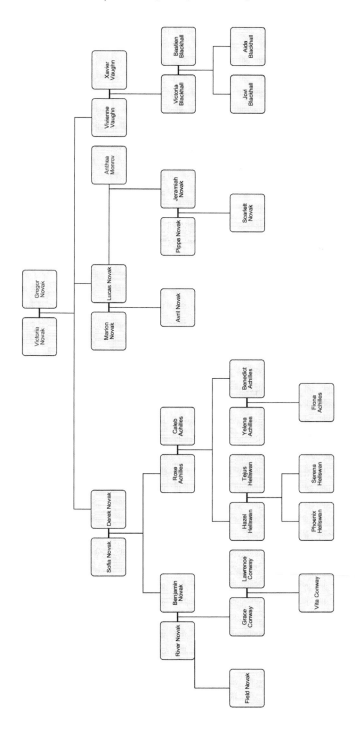